PRAISE FOR THE RADIUM AGE SERIES

"New editions of a host of under-discussed classics of the genre."
—Tor.com

"Neglected classics of early 20th-century sci-fi in spiffily designed paperback editions."
—*The Financial Times*

"An entertaining, engrossing glimpse into the profound and innovative literature of the early twentieth century."
—*Foreword*

"Shows that 'proto-sf' was being published much more widely, alongside other kinds of fiction, before it emerged as a genre."
—*BSFA Review*

"An excellent start at showcasing the strange wonders offered by the Radium Age."
—*Shelf Awareness*

"Lovingly curated . . . The series' freedom from genre purism lets us see how a specific set of anxieties—channeled through dystopias, Lovecraftian horror, arch social satire, and adventure tales—spurred literary experimentation and the bending of conventions."
—*Los Angeles Review of Books*

"A huge effort to help define a new era of science fiction."
—*Transfer Orbit*

"Admirable . . . and highly recommended."
—*Washington Post*

"Long live the Radium Age."
—*Los Angeles Times*

THE INHUMANS AND OTHER STORIES

The Radium Age Book Series
Joshua Glenn

Voices from the Radium Age, edited by Joshua Glenn, 2022
A World of Women, J. D. Beresford, 2022
The World Set Free, H. G. Wells, 2022
The Clockwork Man, E. V. Odle, 2022
Nordenholt's Million, J. J. Connington, 2022
Of One Blood, Pauline Hopkins, 2022
What Not, Rose Macaulay, 2022
The Lost World and The Poison Belt, Arthur Conan Doyle, 2023
Theodore Savage, Cicely Hamilton, 2023
The Napoleon of Notting Hill, G. K. Chesterton, 2023
The Night Land, William Hope Hodgson, 2023
More Voices from the Radium Age, edited by Joshua Glenn, 2023
Man's World, Charlotte Haldane, 2024
The Inhumans and Other Stories: A Selection of Bengali Science Fiction, edited and translated by Bodhisattva Chattopadhyay, 2024

THE INHUMANS AND OTHER STORIES

A SELECTION OF BENGALI SCIENCE FICTION

edited and translated by
Bodhisattva Chattopadhyay

THE MIT PRESS
CAMBRIDGE, MASSACHUSETTS
LONDON, ENGLAND

This edition of *The Inhumans* is translated from the text of the 1935 edition of Hemendrakumar Roy's *Amanushik Manush*, published by Dev Sahitya Kutir, which is in the public domain. Jagadananda Ray's "Voyage to Venus" was translated from the text originally published as "Shukra Bhraman" in *Bharati* in 1895. Manoranjan Bhattacharya's "The Martian Purana" was translated from the text originally published as "Mangal Purana" in *Ramdhanu* in 1931. Nanigopal Majumdar's "The Mystery of the Giant" was translated from the text originally published as "Danab Rahassya" in *Ramdhanu* in 1931.

This book was set in Arnhem Pro and PF DIN Text Pro by New Best-set Typesetters Ltd. Printed and bound in the United States of America.

Library of Congress Cataloging-in-Publication Data

Names: Chattopadhyay, Bodhisattva, editor, translator.
Title: The inhumans and other stories : a selection of Bengali science fiction / edited and translated by Bodhisattva Chattopadhyay.
Description: Cambridge, Massachusetts : The MIT Press, [2024] | Series: The radium age book series | Includes bibliographical references.
Identifiers: LCCN 2023013516 (print) | LCCN 2023013517 (ebook) | ISBN 9780262547611 (paperback) | ISBN 9780262378055 (epub) | ISBN 9780262378048 (pdf)
Subjects: LCSH: Science fiction, Bengali—Translations into English.
Classification: LCC PK1716.5.E5 .I54 2024 (print) | LCC PK1716.5.E5 (ebook) | DDC 808.83/8762089144—dc23/eng/20230628
LC record available at https://lccn.loc.gov/2023013516
LC ebook record available at https://lccn.loc.gov/2023013517

10 9 8 7 6 5 4 3 2 1

CONTENTS

SERIES FOREWORD

Joshua Glenn

Do we really know science fiction? There were the scientific romance years that stretched from the mid-nineteenth century to circa 1900. And there was the genre's so-called golden age, from circa 1935 through the early 1960s. But between those periods, and overshadowed by them, was an era that has bequeathed us such tropes as the robot (berserk or benevolent), the tyrannical superman, the dystopia, the unfathomable extraterrestrial, the sinister telepath, and the eco-catastrophe. A dozen years ago, writing for the sf blog io9.com at the invitation of Annalee Newitz and Charlie Jane Anders, I became fascinated with the period during which the sf genre as we know it emerged. Inspired by the exactly contemporaneous career of Marie Curie, who shared a Nobel Prize for her discovery of radium in 1903, only to die of radiation-induced leukemia in 1934, I eventually dubbed this three-decade interregnum the "Radium Age."

Curie's development of the theory of radioactivity, which led to the extraordinary, terrifying, awe-inspiring insight that the atom is, at least in part, a state of energy constantly in movement, is an apt metaphor for the twentieth century's first three decades. These years were marked by rising sociocultural strife across various fronts: the founding of the women's suffrage movement, the National Association for the Advancement of Colored People, socialist currents within the labor movement, anticolonial and revolutionary upheaval around the world . . . as well as the associated strengthening of reactionary movements that supported, for example, racial segregation, immigration restriction, eugenics, and sexist policies.

Science—as a system of knowledge, a mode of experimenting, and a method of reasoning—accelerated the pace of change during these years in ways simultaneously liberating and terrifying. As sf author and historian Brian Stableford points out in his 1989 essay "The Plausibility of the Impossible," the universe we discovered by means of the scientific method in the early twentieth century defies common sense: "We are haunted by a sense of the impossibility of ultimately making sense of things." By playing host to certain far-out notions—time travel, faster-than-light travel, and ESP, for example—that we have every reason to judge impossible, science fiction serves as an "instrument of negotiation," Stableford suggests, with which we strive to accomplish "the difficult diplomacy of existence in a scientifically knowable but essentially unimaginable world." This is no less true today than during the Radium Age.

The social, cultural, political, and technological upheavals of the 1900–1935 period are reflected in the proto-sf writings of authors such as Olaf Stapledon, William Hope Hodgson, Muriel Jaeger, Karel Čapek, G. K. Chesterton, Cicely Hamilton, W. E. B. Du Bois, Yevgeny Zamyatin, E. V. Odle, Arthur Conan Doyle, Mikhail

Bulgakov, Pauline Hopkins, Stanisław Ignacy Witkiewicz, Aldous Huxley, Gustave Le Rouge, A. Merritt, Rudyard Kipling, Rose Macaulay, J. D. Beresford, J. J. Connington, S. Fowler Wright, Jack London, Thea von Harbou, and Edgar Rice Burroughs, not to mention the late-period but still incredibly prolific H. G. Wells himself. More cynical than its Victorian precursor yet less hard-boiled than the sf that followed, in the writings of these visionaries we find acerbic social commentary, shock tactics, and also a sense of frustrated idealism—and reactionary cynicism, too—regarding humankind's trajectory.

The MIT Press's Radium Age series represents a much-needed evolution of my own efforts to champion the best proto-sf novels and stories from 1900 to 1935 among scholars already engaged in the fields of utopian and speculative fiction studies, as well as general readers interested in science, technology, history, and thrills and chills. By reissuing literary productions from a time period that hasn't received sufficient attention for its contribution to the emergence of science fiction as a recognizable form—one that exists and has meaning in relation to its own traditions and innovations, as well as within a broader ecosystem of literary genres, each of which, as John Rieder notes in *Science Fiction and the Mass Cultural Genre System* (2017), is itself a product of overlapping "communities of practice"—we hope not only to draw attention to key overlooked works but perhaps also to influence the way scholars and sf fans alike think about this crucial yet neglected and misunderstood moment in the emergence of the sf genre.

John W. Campbell and other Cold War–era sf editors and propagandists dubbed a select group of writers and story types from the pulp era to be the golden age of science fiction. In doing so, they helped fix in the popular imagination a too-narrow understanding of what the sf genre can offer. (In his introduction to the 1974 collection *Before the Golden Age*, for example, Isaac Asimov notes that although it may have possessed a certain exuberance, in general sf from before the mid-1930s moment when Campbell assumed editorship of *Astounding Stories* "seems, to anyone who has experienced the Campbell Revolution, to be clumsy, primitive, naive.") By returning to an international tradition of scientific speculation via fiction from after the Poe–Verne–Wells era and before sf's Golden Age, the Radium Age series will demonstrate—contra Asimov et al.—the breadth, richness, and diversity of the literary works that were responding to a vertiginous historical period, and how they helped innovate a nascent genre (which wouldn't be named until the mid-1920s, by Hugo Gernsback, founder of *Amazing Stories* and namesake of the Hugo Awards) as a mode of speculative imagining.

The MIT Press's Noah J. Springer and I are grateful to the sf writers and scholars who have agreed to serve as this series' advisory board. Aided by their guidance, we'll endeavor to surface a rich variety of texts, along with introductions by a diverse group of sf scholars, sf writers, and others that will situate these remarkable, entertaining, forgotten works within their own social, political, and scientific contexts, while drawing out contemporary parallels.

We hope that reading Radium Age writings, published in times as volatile as our own, will serve to remind us that our own era's seemingly natural, eternal, and inevitable social, economic, and cultural forms and norms are—like Madame Curie's atom—forever in flux.

INTRODUCTION: HEMENDRAKUMAR ROY AND BANGLA SF IN THE RADIUM AGE

Bodhisattva Chattopadhyay

A titan of early Bangla popular literature, the Indian Bengali writer Hemendrakumar Roy (1888–1963) adapted a variety of forms to a South Asian sensibility, including detective fiction, for which he is best known, as well as horror, fantasy, children's literature, and science fiction. It is hard to do justice to the astonishing range of Roy's work; his collected works in Bangla are currently published in 27 individual volumes. As a translator and editor, too, he was well-suited to bring the latest works from the rest of the world, especially British, French, and American literature, in Bangla translation via his numerous networks and publications. Like major contemporaries such as Rabindranath Tagore and Premendra Mitra, through all of his writing and translation work Roy engaged in the processes of nation building; his work was imbued with anticolonial sentiment while eschewing the lazy comfort of nationalism. In his adaptations as well as his own work, he emphasized religious and political unity for a nation under stress from both internal religious conflicts and the effect of British imperial "divide-and-rule" policy. Much like sf itself, nation building for Roy constituted a future-oriented activity that could break free from the mythologies of the past, dissect the problems of the present, and offer better values for the time to come. To this end, Roy created enduring characters of Bangla juvenile literature, such as the popular adventure duo Bimal/Kumar and the detective duo Jayanta/Manik, who through their exploits find ways to unite different Indian communities.

Within this context, Roy's *Amaanushik Maanush* (The Inhumans, 1935) is a fascinating novel, presenting to its readers major tropes of early sf from a uniquely Bengali and Indian lens . . . and then setting those tropes on fire via a comical caricature of the superhuman trope.

Written during the last years of British rule in India, Roy's novel occupies a unique place among early magazine sf in Bangla, between the adventure tales that were common fare for the pulps of the era, and the more mature sf that was to emerge in the years following independence. *The Inhumans* follows two major serialized sf novels by Roy: *Meghduter Marte Agaman* (The Arrival of the Messengers from the Skies, 1925–26), and *Maynamatir Mayakanan* (The Enchanted Garden of Maynamati, 1926–27), the former a Martian adventure, and the latter set in a lost world. Both these novels are Bimal/Kumar adventures. However, *The Inhumans* is a standalone work, which gave Roy space to explore the same themes without affecting the chronology of his popular characters.

In its framing, *The Inhumans* utilizes one of the most common adventure/sf tropes of the period: the "Lost Race" adventure. This trope, popularized by the likes of H. G. Wells, H. Rider Haggard, Arthur Conan Doyle, and Edgar Rice Burroughs, was a spin on nineteenth-century geological discoveries, evolutionary theory, and Social movement, Roy was wary of the notion that civilizational progress necessarily meant technological progress, or vice versa. He was just as wary, though, of any form of nationalist jingoism or excess that posited advanced civilizations or races in one's own national past. While the former narrative had to be challenged because of its racist and caricatured representation of the inferiority of the colonized, the latter had to be challenged because of its tendency towards fascism. (Aryan supremacy narratives, seeded from the Indian subcontinent, had become a prominent fascist trope by the 1930s—and had begun to affect the tone of the Indian independence movement, including in Bengal.) Reading this narrative today, at a time of returning nationalist myths in India, Roy appears prescient in his resistance to nationalist mythmaking.

Roy utilizes both adventure and parody for his criticism. While the first quarter of the narrative conjures up the same atmosphere as other lost-race narratives set in Africa (with scenes of hunting, treks through the jungle, and so on, leading all the way to an encounter with a feral human raised by gorillas), the bulk of the novel is set in the land of the Inhumans. These are a lost race of Bengalis, possessing arcane ancient knowledge that makes them technologically and physically evolved supermen . . . and yet theirs is a degenerate society. In his criticism of sf's superman idea, Roy's narrative is a rare example of irony in early Bangla sf. From Jagadananda Ray's "Voyage to Venus" (1895) and Nanigopal Majumdar's "The Mystery of the Giant" (1931), to name two stories also collected in this volume, we typically find Bangla scientific romance and sf taking its subjects—including, in the latter story, characters transformed by arcane science—quite seriously. This is not to suggest that these stories are less worthy of our attention than *The Inhumans*; the point is that they are more typical of early Bangla sf.

Even Premendra Mitra, Roy's contemporary and another titan of Bangla sf, who utilized the Lost World trope in several early fictions, for example the 1928 story "Bhayankar" (Terrifying), rarely utilized parody or satire during this phase of his writing. Mitra, moreover, actively and unironically utilized the trope of the intellectually superior Bengali scientist—and in that his work seems closer to the general tone of the more naive variety of American pulp sf, with its uncritical valorization of science and scientists. Unlike these and other Bangla sf stories from c. 1900–1935, Roy's narrative sharply expresses disenchantment with superman narratives. Even the superman characters in the story who are not evil have a wild, sadistic, or puerile streak—making their other technological or physical abilities a matter of concern rather than one of celebration. Roy's special ire is directed towards the scientist in the story, one whose predilection for corporeal violence—and whose morbid fascination with the biological improvement of a master race—parallels the contemporary career of the Nazi scientist Josef Mengele.

If there is less caricature in any part of Roy's novel, it is in its presentation of the central Bengali adventurer figure. Roy saw physical development as essential to India's nation-building, and in much of his literary work, including in his editorial contributions to the magazine *Rangmashal* (The Torch, 1937–1946), he placed particular emphasis on the physical over the intellectual. Disputing the colonial British stereotype of the effeminate Bengali male, Roy created characters who were intrepid, hypermasculine adventurers who could roam the planet carrying nothing but a rifle. Mitra, as well as later sf writers like Satyajit Ray, depicted Indian scientists and other intellectual figures who stood tall in the company of their European and American peers; by contrast, although Roy's heroes are intelligent they are rarely scientists or armchair intellectuals. Since Bengal had a strong intellectual tradition, the opening lines of *The Inhumans* presents our narrator as a different kind of Bengali—one intended to serve as a role model.

Roy wasn't the only Bengali writer for whom Africa proved a perfect setting to demonstrate a character's masculinity and courage. Bibhutibhushan Bandopadhyay's wildly popular 1937 adventure novel *Chander Pahar* (Mountain of the Moon), for example, also features a Bengali hunter-adventurer in Africa. In setting the action of *The Inhumans* in Africa, Roy was following in the footsteps of popular Anglo-American and European adventure and sf authors; unfortunately, his presentation of the African continent is laced with these writers' same racist biases and tropes. In early European and American sf, meanwhile, in addition to offering a "primitive" backdrop for virile adventurers, Africa served as a sufficiently alien locale for unrestrained speculation about advanced lost races. The two narratives of *The Inhumans*, one concerning an intrepid Bengali hunter and the other a hyper-advanced Bengali scientist, signal these two extremes.

The two main sections of *The Inhumans* are radically different in tone. Whereas the jungles of Africa are treated with reverence, sublimity, and seriousness, the hidden, advanced Bengali civilization is treated with parody, horror, and disdain. Early Bangla sf (like early sf elsewhere) is a volatile admixture of genres. In *The Inhumans* we find folklore and myth (a vector for national ideologies or political belief systems), fable and fantasy (which brings in a speculative element), and also horror (the unexplored and the unexplained within the speculative), all of which are held together by the realistic "glue" of adventure (a genre that encompasses historical romances, geographical tales, and travel narratives). It is thanks mainly to adventure that Bangla sf expresses an aspiration for future possibilities.

These and other genres found expression through literary magazines in colonial Bengal. Magazines such as *Ramdhanu*, *Rangmashal*, *Mouchak*, *Bharati*, and *Sandesh* carried translations, puzzles, short fiction, serialized novels, news of inventions and discoveries, historical articles, stories from mythological sources, geographical pieces, political commentary, and more—all between the same covers. Children's fiction, comedy, fantasy, myth-fiction, and sf could all be found here; the reader picking up a new issue could never be certain of what might be on offer. Alongside original sf, fantasy, and Vernian techno-fiction by writers such as Roy, Mitra, Kshitindranarayan Bhattacharya, Manoranjan Bhattacharya, Charuchandra Chakraborty, Sushilchandra Mitra, Parashuram, and others, these magazines also carried translations or adaptations of Conan Doyle, Wells, Burroughs, and Verne—much of which was translated or adapted by Roy himself.

Within this literary space, genres were as productively mixed-up as in *The Inhumans* itself. For instance in *Rangmashal*, launched in 1937 and edited by Roy, we find Mitra's sf adventure *Prithibi Chariye* (Beyond Earth, 1937) identified simply as a novel, alongside a detective novel, a travelog, word puzzles, and descriptive articles about foreign customs—all clustered within a single category, "Durer Alo" (distant light). While one could argue that this category title makes sense for Mitra's novel, there is no effort to explain why the others belong here. It is therefore no surprise that Bangla sf would emerge within this context as a genre that borrows from travel writing as well as from articles on science, as much for the purpose of entertainment as for education, and offering folklore and myth, fable and fantasy, and horror within an ostensibly realistic "adventure" frame.

This sort of mashup is also noticeable in the shorter works written and published in these magazines. In "Mangal Purana" (The Martian Purana, 1931) by Manoranjan Bhattacharya, which is included in this volume, we find advanced aliens coexisting in the same space as mythological characters. Bhattacharya never seeks to establish the logicality of the extrapolation; his narrative seamlessly accommodates the scientific and the mythic.

Nor does Bhattacharya recognize different orders of time: A "Purana" is a tale that takes place outside of time, yet here the past merges with both the present (via contemporary social and cultural references) and the extrapolated future (via the Martians). By bringing the three time frames together, the mythic is re-enabled as a form of social commentary.

In the context of this undifferentiated genre system, *The Inhumans* makes more sense. While its initial section is a geography lesson, an expedition narrative, and a feral-child campfire tale, the section on the lost civilization is both mythical and futuristic. The lost race has diverged from present-day Bengalis, we learn, during a mythic period of South Asian history, specifically the realm of the legendary founder of Sri Lanka, Prince Vijaya (c. 543–505 BCE). The monarchical political system within the advanced civilization echoes contemporary children's fantasy literature, such as the *Goopy Gyne Bagha Byne* stories by Upendrakishore Ray Chowdhury. And grotesque, shape-shifting beings are central to fairy tales and folk narratives—for instance in stories by Roy's contemporary Dakshinaranjan Mitra Majumdar, who wrote or assembled numerous fairy tale and folklore collections that remain popular. Also relevant here are tall tales, which were exploited for genre purposes in the colonial Bengali context by Trailokyanath Mukhopadhyay in his *Damarudhar* cycle.

What makes *The Inhumans* a unique literary artifact within its context, however, is Roy's use of the scientific to bring folklore, horror, and mythical elements into the realm of advanced knowledge. Readers encountering it for the first time are in for a treat.

Note on the Translation

While *The Inhumans* has never been out of print in Bengal, this is the first English-language translation of the novel, as well as of the three other stories appended to this collection. "Voyage to Venus" is one of the first works of scientific romance in Bangla, appearing in *Bharati* magazine in 1895. The story contains some of the same themes as *The Inhumans* but unfolds as an extraplanetary voyage. "The Mystery of the Giant" (1931) echoes Roy in offering us a glimpse of supermen and their concerns with the physiological improvement of humankind. "The Martian Purana," published in *Ramdhanu* in 1931, is part of the author's cycle of whimsical modern mythological stories. This story also deals with the theme of superhuman aliens and human degeneration—which, when combined with its use of satire, colonial setting, and critical use of myth, makes it a suitable way to round off this showcase of Bangla sf from the Radium Age.

For any translator, the most evocative possible translation of a work's title is crucial, since the title sets the mood. The word অমানুষিক means *inhuman*, while the word মানুষ means *human as individual* but also *humanity*. So the literal translation of the title could be *The Inhuman Humans*, or else *The Inhuman Human*. Given the context of the period, I also considered titles such as *The Supermen*, and also, if one was to be Nietzschean, *The Overmen*. By choosing *The Inhumans*, I wanted to encourage readers to perceive such characters as the feral child, the beings in the advanced civilization, and even the narrators as different sorts of inhumans: the first in animality, the second in their distance from humanity, and the narrators in their violence, which they are eager to inflict on wild animals but unable to accept should it be inflicted upon them by a "superior" species.

While Roy's prose remains quite readable today in its original Bangla, it offers numerous difficulties in translation—for instance, in the translation of songs and rhymes. In my translation, I have emphasized the spirit of the original. I have focused on translation of content, meaning, and affect, rather than simple emphasis on structure. Since Roy's wide corpus of adventure fiction is still untranslated, it was also important for me to find a way to express in modern English what makes him such an enduring (and endearing) writer in his own language, especially how he moves seamlessly between nail-biting tension and whimsy. My hope is that *The Inhumans*, which introduces Roy's sf to English-speaking readers outside Bengal, will serve as a gateway to further translations of his work.

Bibliography

Arvidsson, Stefan. *Aryan Idols: Indo-European Mythology as Ideology and Science*. Trans. Sonia Wichmann. Chicago: University of Chicago Press, 2006.

Ballantyne, Tony. *Orientalism and Race: Aryanism in the British Empire*. Hampshire, UK: Palgrave Macmillan, 2002.

Chattopadhyay, Bodhisattva. "Kalpavigyan and Imperial Technoscience: Three Nodes of an Argument." *Journal of Fantastic in the Arts*, vol. 28 no. 1 (2018): 102–122.

Chattopadhyay, Bodhisattva. “Hemendrakumar Ray and the Birth of Adventure Kalpabigyan.” *JU Essays and Studies* vol. 18 (2013): 35–54.

Ghosh, Ranen. “Travelling in a Time Machine to the Golden Age of Science Fiction in Kolkata: (1963–1985).” In *Matti Braun*, edited by Matti Braun, Bodhisattva Chattopadhyay, and Beth Citron, 83–90. Cologne: Snoeck, 2020.

Greenslade, William. *Degeneration, Culture and the Novel: 1880–1940.* Cambridge: Cambridge University Press, 1994.

Hurley, Kelly. *The Gothic Body: Sexuality, Materialism and Degeneration at the* Fin-de-siècle. Cambridge: Cambridge University Press, 1996.

Rieder, John. *Colonialism and the Emergence of Science Fiction.* Middletown, CT: Wesleyan University Press, 2008.

Satadru, Sen. “A Juvenile Periphery: The Geographies of Literary Childhood In Colonial Bengal.” *Journal of Colonialism and Colonial History*, vol. 5 no. 1 (2004). https://doi.org/10.1353/cch.2004.0039.

Trautmann, Thomas R. *Aryans and British India.* Berkeley: University of California Press, 1997.

THE INHUMANS (1935)

Hemendrakumar Roy

1 The Hunter's Heaven

Mechanical automobiles, ships, airships, and airplanes have given us access to the whole planet. Geography textbooks have taught us all we need to know. Life has even been detected on Mars and other worlds. Scholars believe they know everything under the sun.

I have no intention of challenging such scholars. I just believe that there are uncharted countries and kingdoms outside the purview of our geography textbooks. I would be immensely thankful if our instructors would first listen to this unusual history before attacking me with their sticks. The authenticity of an oral narrative may be contested, but it cannot be completely disregarded.

Bengalis are notorious for laziness. This is not a matter of choice but rather of necessity. While other Indians are eager to leave the country for a better life, we Bengalis have inflated self-esteem. The Odias[1] feel no shame in driving cabs, tending gardens, or waiting tables. The Marwaris[2] have no qualms about selling ghee pots, garments, or dishes on the streets of Kolkata. Many labor contentedly as coolies in Fiji, Africa, or South America. This is what Bengalis cannot do. We get offended when asked to do menial work. While others don't hesitate to stoop first for the promise of prosperity, Bengalis don't bow our heads to foreigners easily for future prospects. Be a door-to-door salesman? Work as a coolie? For shame! This is the Bengali mentality. To maintain our self-respect, we would even embrace the reputation of being lazy.

So I wasn't surprised that there weren't many Bengalis among the many Indians in Africa. The majority of Indians here do not have gentlemanly occupations. Why would Bengalis mix with such a bunch?

You may wonder why I, a Bengali, was in Africa. This may come as a surprise, but I didn't come here to work as a shopkeeper, a coolie, or even for a job. I came here to hunt. Oh how I love to hunt. I have the means, the time, and the liberty to devote myself to my obsession. I have taken every sort of large game in India's woods and jungles. I have collected it all. So I came to Africa in good faith to see whether the hippopotamuses, gorillas, and lions would prove worthy of my effort in hunting them.

India is renowned for its tigers, elephants, cobras, and other ferocious creatures. For hunters worldwide, our Sundarbans are comparable to paradise; I have spent many joyful and wonderful years in these mangrove forests. I shall never forget their many marshes, uncountable streams and ponds, deep and dark woods, deserted sandy beaches, the scent of moist earth, and the beauty of their isolation. There, the water crocodile lashes its tail in frustration at the arboreal python. There in the undergrowth, a Bengal tiger moves as swiftly as lightning. There, noxious marsh vapors or dense mists rise slowly over the Sundari trees, obscuring the whole sky. No respectable hunter would consider his or her life complete without visiting the Sundarbans.

But Africa, with its huge woods, is an even greater hunting paradise. The Sundarbans dwarf in comparison to such vast wilderness. The ferocious lion, king of creatures, hippo, elephant, rhino, giraffe, zebra, cheetah, leopard, panther, gorilla, baboon, chimpanzee, mandrill, boar, gnu, camels, ostrich, okapi, wild buffalo, several species of deer, apes, and crocodiles—Africa is a menagerie. There is nowhere else on Earth where one may find such a variety of wild creatures. The gorilla, lion, and hippopotamus are the three species that I was most excited to collect. With civilizational progress, it has become possible to travel to the darkest depths of Africa. Large automobiles race across the beautiful roads that curve through these woodlands. It now takes three months to experience what used to take three years. Thanks to all the motorcars on land and all the motorboats on water, the thrill of risk at every step, which used to make hunters' hearts sing with joy, is now much diminished. These days a few "hunters" even fly to Africa in order to obtain their trophies. What possible satisfaction could they derive from such a stunt? They could just as easily go and shoot some caged tigers, lions, and hippos at a zoo. The hunt without its inherent perils is not worthy of the name!

However, even in the twenty-first century, one cannot drive a motorcar through the Congolese jungles. So I hired several coolies and attendants to carry my equipment, and we set off on foot into the wilderness, leaving civilization behind. If I were to fall victim to a lion, hippo, or gorilla, I wanted it to be a worthwhile goodbye.

In the course of our expedition, we came upon Lake Bunyonyi.[3] Its pristine blue waters with gorgeous reeds jutting out here and there towards the edges, and its magnificent pink-lavender lotuses floating above the blue like a still-life painting . . . no language has the vocabulary to express the magnificence of this scene. India does not have such enormous lotuses. These are at least ten feet broad, and the stalks are as robust as cords made from coconut fiber. Flowering euphorbias grow along the lake's dark, elevated shores.

Although Bengal's wildness is also gorgeous, it is not as unusual as this. There are mountains, volcanoes, waterfalls, and lakes in these parts that cannot be found in the Sundarbans. Every step here leads to fresh adventures and wonders. We have spent days traversing this woodland on foot, but I am not tired in the least due to its unending diversity. Yet despite all this beauty, there remains a sense of dread, a shadow of abrupt, unforeseen disaster. If one wants to wax lyrical about all the glories, one must do so with great caution, since the slightest negligence might result in disaster.

One night, we camped beside a river. Due to our extreme fatigue from the day's hike and the dense darkness of the evening, we were negligent about where we pitched our tents. Even now, I shudder when I recall what transpired due to such a minor error.

We finished dining early, and I fell asleep as soon as I lay down on the camp-cot. Having spent most of my life on expeditions, I was used to sleeping well under any circumstances.

I do not recall how long I'd slept, but I do remember waking up in the midst of a pleasant dream. Half-asleep, I heard a tremendous commotion outside my tent. By the time I'd become more alert, the noise had subsided. I started to question whether it had just been a dream, but further events shattered this assumption. I was startled by a bizarre, very loud grunting sound right next to me!

I swiftly lit my flashlight and directed it toward the sound. I could only see the flapping of my tent's walls. Then I heard the sound again, this time coming from the other side. Again, just the flapping of the walls could be heard. What might this be? What was this noise? What was causing these walls to flap? As I lay there startled, sounds began to emanate from all directions, and the walls began to sway violently.

I snatched up my weapon in a split second. Who was making so much noise outside, and why? What did they want?

I can't recall exactly what transpired next. It resembled a tremor or maybe an avalanche. Suddenly, everything started to tremble, and I was violently projected from my tent.

Had it been anybody else, they would have likely fainted by that point, but I have been exposed to peril for many years and have often looked death in the face. Though I was bruised and disoriented, I sat up as soon as I struck the ground. In the low light of the moon, I saw several colossal white creatures walking past, shaking the ground as they passed. Though I looked up and down, left and right, I could not see my tent anywhere.

Forcing myself to get up and hobbling a few steps, I saw shattered bits of wood and torn rags strewn about—the only remnants of my tent. I'd had nearly thirty coolies and porters with me as well, but they seem to have been melted into air by some magical mantra. While I was contemplating, I heard some ominous noises in the distance—so I hurriedly climbed a massive tree next to me.

Imagine my amazement when I realized that the creatures were merely hippos. They smelled the ruins of the tent cautiously as they got nearer, and when they found nothing, they went back to the river. Everything made sense now. Every wild animal follows a certain route to the nearest water source—and the passage for hippos was where we had stupidly pitched our tents.

Hippos are renowned for their obstinacy and strength, but also for their idiocy. Two hippos were approaching the river when they encountered my tent. My men had fled in terror at the sight of them. Puzzled by this odd construction in the middle of nowhere, the hippos had pushed and butted the tent from all sides as though it were a wild animal invading their territory. The tent had crumbled as they'd attacked it, trapping them in the tangle of rope and wood. So they'd flung what parts of it they could around the campsite before fleeing with the remainder.

Every step you take in the wilderness is fraught with peril. Those who have never experienced it have no way of knowing just how perilous it really is; make a single mistake and you may never have a chance to make another. It would not be out of place here to mention the tragic tale of Paul Graetz, a German officer who went to hunt wild buffalo in Africa.[4] No one should laugh when they think of the buffalo. Some hunters even go so far as to consider the wild buffalo more dangerous than predators like lions and tigers, so it is safe to say that they are not easy prey.

The incident is mentioned in the book *Kill or Be Killed*, by Major W. Robert Foran.[5] Listen to this tale from Graetz himself, since such stories of dangers faced while hunting are indeed rare:

> I was then traveling in Rhodesia along Lake Bangweolo in a launch [the *Sarotti*]. In my team, I had a French cinematograph operator, Octave Fière, an African cook named James, and four other African natives. [. . .]
>
> The tales I had heard of Lake Bangweolo from the Awemba tribe, on my former motor-car journey across Africa, had made me most anxious to explore this mysterious sheet of water in the heart of North-Eastern Rhodesia. According to them, this lake enjoyed a most sinister reputation among the native tribes residing both near and far. They declared that it was studded with islands, on which were to be found mammoth elephants and immense giraffes; while in its waters were huge sea-serpents and other strange creatures. From the surface, hot springs rose like fountains into the air; and pestilential winds, sweeping across the nearby swamps, carried death to all who ventured near the lake's shores. I gathered from the Awemba that

Bangweolo and its vicinity was no health resort: rather a Dante's Inferno.

These people insisted that no natives, who had ever ventured upon the waters of this lake in their frail canoes, had again been seen or heard of: they had just vanished. Bangweolo was regarded by some local tribes as a sort of Hades, where departed souls suffered continually the most dreadful torments; while others again believed it was the approach to a Paradise, where the spirits of their dead relatives enjoyed a perfect life under the benign protection of their gods.

After making all due allowances for their imagination and local native superstitions, Lake Bangweolo sounded sinister but worth investigating.

The lake was known to be surrounded by miles upon miles of thick and impenetrable marshes, and the swamps thickly clothed with tall papyrus reeds and rushes. This all rendered any chance of exploring its waters a matter of great difficulty. But the more obstacles placed in my path, the more I looked forward to the adventure. Any expedition into unknown regions would be deadly tame and devoid of all pleasurable thrills if all was smooth sailing. I was perfectly well aware that we should have to endure many severe hardships and swallow many keen disappointments; but what of that? No adventure is worth calling such unless it possesses those two characteristics.

The great prize which I hoped to secure, in addition to being the first white man to thoroughly explore this sheet of water in the wild heart of Africa, was one or more specimens of a giant buffalo, reported by the Awemba to make its home on the marshy shores of the lake. They had assured me that these colossal beasts were unusually fierce and dangerous. From all I was told, they seemed to be a new species of African buffalo.

We set off from Quelimane with light hearts and filled with hope. Mile after mile we journeyed onwards. Everything went according to plan, and the river journey proved quite uneventful. The *Sarotti* behaved beautifully, and fully justified the care I had devoted to its design. We were a very happy party, and enjoyed every minute of our adventure until we made the difficult passage of the watershed to Fife, over the so-called Stevenson Road. This was no road at all, in the generally accepted meaning of that word. After several weary weeks of hard labor in a terrific tropical heat, we managed to push the launch on its specially designed wheeled-carriage across the watershed, and reached the banks of the Chambezi River.

Even when the little *Sarotti* once more floated on the waters of this river, our trials were not ended. The next phase of the journey to Bangweolo was full of dangers, unexpected and impossible to guard against. The river had never before been navigated by anything larger than an African's canoe; it was uncharted, and full of snags and sandbanks; and the hippo daily threatened our small craft with disaster. These brutes seemed to have a passion for bumping us or else trying to climb on board. As we slowly voyaged down the river, our hearts were often in our mouths.

Comparatively speaking, all went well with us until we had almost reached the shores of Bangweolo. Then disaster, dire and dreadful, overtook and swamped us. Within sight of our goal, we were overcome by a cruel and relentless fate.

At dawn, one morning, the blood-red sun of a new day rose triumphantly over the crest of the dark chain of the Muchemwa Mountains, drenching the countryside in vivid coloring. It bade us rise, and continue our journey down the Chambezi to our longed-for destination. The sun melted the mists on the river's surface; and at our feet, as we emerged from our tent on the bank, lay our little motor-boat. It was anchored in a small bay formed by a deep bend in the river's course.

A deep peace and stillness pervaded everything; but in Africa things happen so quickly, that there is seldom any real warning of approaching danger. One moment all is happiness and contentment: the next, you are battling for your life against some wholly unexpected terror. Little did we know, as we stood on the bank of the river and watched the beauties of the gorgeous sunrise, what that day held in store for us. Perhaps it was well that we were unable to gaze into the mirror of life.

As the sun rose in the sky, we embarked on the launch. A few moments later, we were being rowed lustily down the Chambezi towards Bangweolo, for whenever possible we conserved our petrol and oil supplies. For a time, nothing unusual occurred. There was no sign of life, except occasional birds and monkeys, along the river's banks. At last, a convenient place to land and have breakfast was seen, and I ran the launch into the bank. While our servants made preparations for the meal, Fière and I rested while lazily smoking and watching the deft handiwork of James in the camp kitchen. Then he called out that our breakfast was ready. We rose, gleefully, to take our seats at the camp table.

As we stood erect, both were petrified with astonishment. Not more than fifty feet from us, and close to the river bank, stood three mighty buffalo of unusual size. They were staring at us with wondering eyes, and perfectly motionless. They had appeared so suddenly and silently through the reeds and bush that nobody had any warning of their approach.

And these were no ordinary buffalo. They were simply gigantic, and suggested to my mind a type of prehistoric animal.

Silence, deep and impressive, reigned for a brief moment or two. It was like the silence that foreshadows death, when the whole world and life seem to stop breathing momentarily. And then I awoke to the extremity of the danger that threatened us. With almost automatic precision, I unslung my rifle from my shoulder, and Fière followed my example.

I fired the instant my cheek rested on the butt of my Mauser rifle and the sights came on my target. *Bang!* The shot ran out, awakening the bird life. The report echoed through the trees to the distant mountain range, and then came back faintly to us.

The leading buffalo stumbled and fell forward on his knees, rose again, shook his ponderous head in mingled pain and shock, and then galloped up the river bank and out of sight into the bush. The other two followed in his wake.

Meanwhile, Fière stood ready to shoot in case of necessity; but there was no further need now. Intermittently, through the dense undergrowth, we caught glimpses of the shaggy forms of the three buffalo as they followed the course of the river toward the lake. Presently, we could see only two of them.

What had become of the third we asked ourselves? We were not yet out of danger, apparently. Possibly the wounded buffalo would return to attack us; but equally well it might be that the three were still together, and we could only see two of them. After a short period of thought, I decided that it was probable that the wounded beast had left his companions. That would be a sure indication that he was badly wounded. If this was so, it would be splendid. We should be able to secure that trophy, after a long pursuit. *Bos caffer graetzii* would read well in the natural history records of African fauna, I thought to myself!

The decision to follow up and kill the wounded giant was soon made. Breakfast was forgotten. Leaving James and two of our natives to clear away the untasted meal and pack the launch ready for a renewed start down the river, Fière and I hastened off on the trail of the buffalo.

It was not difficult to follow. Large smears of blood were seen everywhere—on bushes, boulders, grass and leaves. I must have hit that buffalo pretty hard.

Judging by that bloody trail. The spoor led up the bank of the Chambezi, and patently the wounded animal was headed for the shelter of the papyrus reeds around Lake Bangweolo. If so, we should gaze upon that most mysterious lake before we had expected.

Hour after hour passed, and still we kept doggedly on the trail of the beast. The sun climbed higher into the sky until it stood directly over our heads, scorching us and everything with its fierce rays; but we were far too intent on our quarry to pay heed to the trials of terrific heat or the rough going. We were obsessed with the lust to kill this new species of African mammoth. Until we had done so, we could know no rest of body or mind. What we had wounded, we must now kill.

At last, after over six hours of fruitless search, nature demanded a temporary halt and rest. The afternoon was well advanced, and we felt ravenous for neither had eaten since dinner on the previous evening. I decided to have the launch brought up to us, and sent back one of our native followers to tell James to come on up the river to the spot where we had halted. We reclined in the shade and rested, waiting for the launch to arrive with something to eat and drink.

An hour before sundown, the motor-boat reached us, and James got busy with the preparation of a much-needed meal. We watched his work with hungry anticipation. Breakfast, lunch, and tea must be merged into one meal.

While the repast was being prepared, I sent three of our natives to search further for the wounded buffalo.

I felt quite positive that he must be lying up in thick cover somewhere in our neighborhood; and I wanted this specimen—and was determined to get it. I offered a liberal reward in cash if they located the beast for me. With this incentive, they hurried off into the dense bush.

We had just finished our meal when they came running back with word that the wounded giant had been found. He was lying down in the long grass near the riverbank, not far from where we then were. We had hoped for some such kind of luck, but had scarcely expected to find it so soon. Fière and I rose excitedly to our feet and got our rifles ready. We were only just in time, for a second later the tall grass parted in front of us, and the buffalo dashed out straight at us.

We both fired simultaneously, so that the two gun reports sounded as one. Having shot, I sprang to one side to avoid that infuriated charge of the beast. As I did so, my foot caught in a tree-root, hidden in the long grass, and I fell forward on to my knees. This accident proved my salvation. If I had remained erect, I must have been impaled upon the sharp and cruel points of the buffalo's wide-sweeping horns.

Snorting with intense anger, the huge animal nosed under me as I fell forward on the ground. He tried hard to toss me into the air on those wicked horns, but failed to get a hold of my body. At last, I sprang to my feet and clung with all my strength to the horns. I hoped that, severely wounded as the beast was, he might give way to me or that Fière could get a chance for a safe shot. For a brief moment or two, which seemed like hours, the buffalo and I pitted our strength against each other. The huge beast was rapidly tiring from loss of blood, and I made a supreme effort to throw him to the ground or, at least, hold him so that Fière might deliver the death-shot. But I was no match for that brute's terrific strength, and there came no shot from my companion.

It all happened in a brief second or two. The buffalo tried to shake off my grip on his horns and, as he flung his massive head from side to side, the point of the left horn pierced deep into my right cheek. I cried out in agony, and then felt myself lifted bodily off the ground and hurled skywards. I remember nothing further of what happened. It was just as well that Nature had dropped a curtain over that scene and blotted out the ghastliness of it all.

In the meantime, I learned afterwards, Fière had come gallantly to my aid, wholly unmindful of his own great danger. It was some time before he could manage to shoot without the risk of hitting me instead of the buffalo. As I was flung away, he fired; but only succeeded in wounding and making the beast more infuriated than ever. The savage brute turned upon Fière instantly, and tossed him again and again. His body was fearfully torn and gored. Then, as if worn out with his terrific vengeance, the buffalo toppled over dead beside our mangled and unconscious bodies.

I recovered my senses to find myself covered with blood and racked by an extremity of pain. I was stretched out on the bank of the river, with the motor-boat afloat below me, being supported in the arms of two of the native followers. Another man was washing my dreadful wounds with cool water.

"Where is the other *Bwana*?" I managed to whisper. The effort was so terribly painful that I almost swooned again.

"The others are bringing him here. He will die soon," answered one of the men sadly.

"And the buffalo?"

"Dead!" came the laconic reply.

A flood of thick blood was flowing continuously from my mouth and the right side of my face. The two natives lifted me gently, to carry me back to the tent which had been erected on the bank; but, with every movement, the blood flowed faster and the pain was excruciating.

"Quick!" I managed to gasp out. "Bring the medicine-chest!"

They brought it. There was only one thing to do, and that quickly. Sew, sew, sew! Terrible necessity taught me how to ply that surgical needle and thread. With a native holding up my shaving-mirror, and another supporting me from behind, I thrust the needle through the raw flesh. A jagged, irregular hole, as large as my hand, gaped in my right cheek; and my under-lip hung down loosely, quivering. Under the horrified stare of the natives, I jabbed the curved needle again and again through my flesh. Somehow I managed to cobble up the tattered ends.

The pain was terrific. Heaven alone helped me to keep my senses and carry on with the ghastly torture of the self-inflicted surgery. My whole being was in revolt, and I was feeling a deadly sickness. To this day, I do not know how it was possible for me to have completed that operation on myself. But it got done, somehow: and more or less efficiently.

My lower jaw was fractured in two different places: near the ear, and near the lips. From this crushed mass, a long splinter of bone, with three teeth attached, hung loosely by the nerves and flesh of the gums. The whole outer flesh of my lower jaw had been scraped loose from the bone. Teeth, roots and bones showed white and shimmering through the awful cavity in my cheek. My tongue had been pierced by the point of the buffalo's horn, and half torn from its roots. I spat out, continually, large and small splinters of bone and broken teeth.

The operation completed to the best of my ability, I made the best job I could of bandaging my face. A strong neat brandy put new life into me, and furnished the necessary strength to face that other surgical operation for poor Fière.

While I had been cobbling up my tattered face, James had prepared a bed in the tent for each of us. When I reached them, he had cut away Fière's clothes with a pair of scissors and had him ready for me to do what I could for the fearful wounds. As I staggered to his side, Fière regained consciousness. Softly his white lips framed two words: "*Très mauvais*!"

A rapid survey of his mangled body showed me at once that his case was quite hopeless. I gave him a stiff injection of morphia, and then set to work to make him as comfortable as I could. I knew he had no possible chance of living for long, and my efforts were directed to easing his pain.

He had been tossed and pierced by those sharp-pointed horns no less than three times. His left breast muscle hung loose with a flap of raw flesh; his heart and lungs, happily, had not touched; and, in his left side, between heart and hip, was a ghastly tear of considerable extent. I sewed up this wound at once and then did what little I could for the others.

When I had completed my rough surgery, James washed, bandaged and put Fière to bed. I was feeling far too weak, sick at all I had seen and had had to do, and too full of pain to be capable of doing any more for my poor companion. Fière was now breathing regularly, and appeared to be sleeping. As I sat on my bed, watched and listened, I began to entertain hopes that he might just pull through the crisis and eventually recover.

Night fell, dark and dismal. It was a night filled with torturing pain, during which my mouth seemed to be filled with red-hot coals. Toward morning, a short and troubled sleep gave me a temporary measure of relief from the awful torments I had to endure. With the gray light of dawn, I awoke to fresh agonies and found everything deathly still about me.

I summoned our servants by clapping my hands together. I could not shout, or do more than whisper softly. Even that effort made me feel sick and faint from the terrible pain the slight movement occasioned.

They came and opened the door of the tent. Fortified by another strong drink of neat brandy, I arose painfully and slowly from the bed, and staggered over to Fière. The first light of a new day fell on a white and shrunken face. I knew at once that he was dead, and freed from all earthly pains. In my heart, I envied him.

So, on the very threshold of success, one was taken and the other left a shattered wreck of a man. It was cruel hard luck!

I instructed James to make arrangements to bury poor Fière's body near our camp, and then to send off a man to Kasama, in North-Eastern Rhodesia, to bring succor. This was the nearest point where any Europeans could be found. And thus, far from all medical aid and alone with my native servants, I faced the grim situation with the best fortitude I could summon to my help.

Dr. G. F. Randall, the District Surgeon, and Mr. Cookson, the District Magistrate, marched day and night for two days to my assistance. But those four to five days of waiting can better be imagined than told in cold words. They were a never-ending nightmare of excruciating bodily pain and grievous mental torture.

Randall performed further surgical operations upon me, and under the most difficult circumstances, in order that I could be moved. And then, on an improvised stretcher, I was carried back to Kasama. That journey was sheer agony to my tortured body, and rendered all the more tragic because of the death of Fière.

With the sad procession was carried the body of my late companion, and Cookson arranged for temporary burial at Charenama; but, later, his body was taken to Kasama and buried there by the White Fathers of the Roman Catholic Mission.

For many weeks I was most carefully nursed back to health and strength at Kasama. When fit to travel, I came on up to Dar-es-Salaam for additional operations in the hospital.

That giant buffalo has turned my face into a caricature of what it was once. I can never look the same again, and must always carry these dreadful scars.

As I already mentioned Major W. Robert Foran earlier, I mention here his own exciting description of the terrible nature of the wild buffalo. Goes without saying that this too is a true story, and once again, from Africa:

My attention was suddenly attracted by a furious commotion in the bush, a short distance ahead of my trail. Advancing silently and cautiously, my ears were assailed by a succession of fierce snarls and deep grunts, a few angry bellows, and then the deep-throated roar of a lion. I could now hear a terrific struggle in progress, and broke into a trot to reach the scene of the conflict as soon as possible. Hamisi [bin Baraka, my brave and trusted gun-bearer,] trotted close to my elbow.

We arrived at the edge of an open space in the dense thorn-scrub, and came abruptly to a halt. So astonished was I at what met my eyes, that my rifle was not even remembered. I felt unable to do anything but stare, with eyes starting out of my head. I could neither move nor speak. Hamisi crept up to my side, and I heard him utter a deep grunt of mingled surprise and pleasure.

Before our eyes, in full view, was a huge black-maned lion and a gigantic bull buffalo engaged in mortal combat. Patently, it was kill or be killed. I would have given a very great deal to have had a movie-camera with me or even a Kodak; but I had left the latter in my camp. What a stupendous opportunity missed! Never again shall I ever again get a sight to equal it; and I had not even a camera.

A camera-lens I would have used gladly on that madly fighting, savage pair of primitive animals; but a rifle—nothing could induce me. I would act as an audience: but shoot I would not. I wanted to see this thing through to a finish, and satisfy my curiosity as to which would prove the victor.

In all my long and varied experience of wildlife, I had only once, that time in India, seen anything so thrilling or more wonderful. Then it was a cow buffalo and a tiger: now a bull and a lion.

I do not know how long that fight had raged before I came accidentally upon the arena. It was obvious that I was only watching the final stages. I have no idea how long I stood there, eyes following intently every single detail of that fierce I lost all count of time.

The lion was firmly fixed on the massive shoulders of the old buffalo when I reached the spot. He was fighting, clawing, biting, and growling ferociously. The buffalo was using all his strength and every cunning ruse to dislodge the antagonist, and get in some deadly work with its powerful head and cruel horns.

Once he did succeed in throwing the lion from his back to the ground; and, before his foe could recover, had driven one horn clean through the body and impaled the beast to the earth. They fought and struggled violently, roaring and bellowing savagely. The whole veld seemed to vibrate to their noisy throats. It was awe-inspiring; and swift thrills ran up and down my spine.

Somehow, the lion managed to free himself. Before he did so, however, he had scored the body of the buffalo in the most terrible fashion. Shreds of hide and flesh were hanging down in long strips, blood and dust were everywhere as they waltzed round and round each other, heads always facing, eyes watchfully intent and glaring, and muscles tensely drawn. Both waited for a favorable moment to spring in again to close grips. Round and round they went, wounds completely ignored or forgotten, frothing with blood at mouth and nostrils, bodies torn open and pouring out a steady stream of scarlet life's blood.

Unexpectedly, almost when I thought the lion had had enough and would slink away to lick his wounds, badly whipped, he sprang in like a flash of lightning and once more landed squarely on the broad shoulders of the buffalo. He perched on neck and withers, his tawny body outstretched along the buffalo's back. The agility of that spring was simply amazing.

It seemed to me that now the buffalo's days were nearly ended, and the fight just about finished. The lion would bite into that massive neck, reach the spinal vertebrae, and with one claw wrench round that great head to breaking point; and then the huge beast would be thrown to death with a broken neck. It is the lion's way of killing big animals.

For a brief second only, I fingered my rifle; but quickly banished all thoughts of intervention. The fight was no concern of mine. Jungle laws had ordained it, and no human being had any shadow of right to interfere. Let the victor not be robbed of the honors in such a gigantic trial of strength.

Now the buffalo was down on his knees, but still struggled valiantly to throw off his foe. They fought all over the arena, savagely and with grim determination. Then, with a swift movement the buffalo threw himself over sideways, and for a moment I thought the lion had actually broken his neck. I was mistaken. The buffalo rolled over the lion, and rose to his feet, freed of that death-hold.

The lion was at him again almost before the buffalo had regained his feet. This time he landed sideways on the shoulder and neck of the bull, just behind that magnificent sweep of horns. He clung there, biting savagely, while the buffalo moaned aloud in agony. But the gallant old beast was not licked: far from it. He fought back strenuously and struggled hard to shake off the lion's tenacious hold. Then, gathering all his strength in a last supreme effort, he threw himself backwards. The lion's body was swung over his head in a half-circle, and he fell on his back beneath that gigantic and heavy body. His tawny hide was lost to view, crushed to a pulp beneath that great bulk of meat and bone.

All round them, the place was a shambles; blood was everywhere. For a moment or two neither animal moved: they appeared to be at death's door. I waited and watched, wondering what the final curtain would be. For a brief instant I turned to look at Hamisi's face. It was streaked with rivers of sweat, eyes staring fixedly, lips parted, and breath coming in gasps. He was hypnotized, oblivious to all but that titanic fight. My eyes swung back to the two combatants.

Slowly and groggily, the buffalo bull staggered to his feet, and stood staring down at the gored and crushed body of his foe. It remained there on the ground, motionless. With two or three savage lunges with those cruel horns into the prostrate body of the Kon, the latter died. The buffalo stood erect over the vanquished, swaying drunkenly on his feet. His eyes were glazing fast; breath coming in short and strangled sobs.

A moment or two of tense silence passed, and still the buffalo swayed on his feet. There was neither sound nor movement, except that terribly labored breathing and that gentle rocking to and fro. The veld all around the arena was as silent as the grave; not even a bird chirped in the nearby trees. I could hear my own heart pumping furiously.

In silence life slipped from the buffalo almost like a smothered sigh. He crumbled slowly, to fall with a dull thud on top of his enemy.

We left them there, victor and vanquished, just as they had fallen.

To have acted otherwise would have been sacrilege.

2 The Night Guest

Hunting gorillas piqued my curiosity more than hunting lions did. There is a plethora of lions in Africa's jungles, and there are many who have hunted lions by the dozen. But gorillas are a rarer species. You won't get to see many gorillas in zoos throughout the world. There are not that many in Africa either, numerically. Furthermore, their great strength and intelligence is unrivaled in the animal kingdom, so most hunters steer clear of these animals.

The forests of Kivu are the home of the gorillas. I have arrived here finally with all my people. The villagers have dubbed a little ditch where water flows freely the 'death ditch.' I had no way of finding out why it bore such a nasty moniker. Close to this ditch there is a large bamboo grove, which is known as Rugano. This is where I first tracked a gorilla's footprints.

Young bamboo shoots are a favorite food of gorillas. The grove extends for kilometers, while three volcanoes, Mikeno, Karisimbi, and Bisoke, stand in the distance. The bamboo trees have taken over even these mountains. The trees are so closely packed together that passing through them requires chopping the plants or crawling through the vegetation. Nettles, red-white fuchsias, balsam plants bearing flowers, veronicas, and purple, yellow, and pink orchids flourish on the forest floor under the towering trees.

There are gorillas, hippos, and buffalo in these woods. There are also cheetahs and other ferocious beasts. When foraging for food, gorillas go from one patch of bamboo to another. Even though they resemble humans, they are not civilized; hence, they do not need to worry about food or labor for a livelihood. There's a plant—break it and eat it. There's water in the pond—drink it. Then make yourself a bed with broken branches and leaves, and sleep and snore contentedly. Oh, how blissful their lives are!

In Kivu, there are two species of plants that are noteworthy. The first is the plant known locally as Musungura. It has tiny, delicate leaves and blooms yellow rose-like flowers. It is about 50 to 60 feet tall. The second plant is called Mugesi. Its leaves resemble those of the walnut and it grows about 100 feet higher. In March and April, it produces dense clusters of violet-magenta blooms. In addition, the lovely orchids are situated on this bed of green and yellow algae. Oh, what a wonderful sight it was to see so many lovely wildflowers. This is a flower-filled land! However, I am traversing this kingdom of flowers armed not with a journal for penning poetry, but with a lethal weapon.

There is one factor that makes gorilla-hunting simpler than lion- or tiger-hunting. It is difficult to spot lions or tigers, but gorillas are relatively simple to locate in their native habitat. This is because they live in packs. They are so powerful that I doubt even lions would have a chance against them, and when they reside in groups, even elephants are no match for them. Gorillas are fully aware of their power, so when an adversary attempts to catch a peek of them, they often do not even bother to pay attention. If they spot a lion or a person from a distance, they will ignore it and then, upon approach, they will aggressively bare their teeth to frighten off their opponents. Those who move closer, however, will suffer a horrifying end. Gorillas like to live their lives quietly and peacefully, and they seldom move quickly or agitate their massive bodies unless the threat is imminent. Therefore, gorillas are simpler to hunt than other animals.

I was also amazed to encounter an unfamiliar kind of human in the Kivu forest. If you were to refer to them in English, I suppose you would use the term "pygmy," but I like to refer to them as Valakhilyas.[6] There are no smaller people on the planet than these Valakhilyas. They are no higher than my waist, and if you see them from a distance, you would imagine them to be a group of children nine or ten years old.

The Valakhilyas have exceptionally dark complexion, curly hair, and flat noses. They wear nothing save an oil-soaked rag to cover their bodies. Despite their small stature, they are very robust, with muscles showing all over their bodies. They are also quite courageous. They take small spears into the thick forests to hunt elephants and the enormous buffalo. Their sole source of livelihood is hunting. They typically subsist on vegetables and roots, but when they are in the mood for meat, they hunt boars and deer with spears and bows and arrows. They do not intermarry with other African tribes. Along the woodland lakes, they dwell in little, idyllic huts covered in leaves. They have no interest in civilization.

While hiking one day I stumbled upon some large beds on the ground—I counted thirty. The beds were constructed with twigs and leaves. The chief of the coolies explained that these were gorilla beds. "I have heard that they never use the same bed twice," I said. "Is that so?" He told me that it was so—and that they must be nearby.

I glanced in every direction. The bamboo and other plants shimmered on the grass below. The branches of the trees were covered in ravens, woodpeckers, doves, sunbirds, and a kind of sparrow. Their songs blended with the murmur of the forest. Sometimes one could see golden monkeys as they ran through the tall forest trees. On the other side a small river flowed in shining silvery waves. It was not long before sunset. I heard the noise of some branches breaking not far from us. I asked the chief coolie again about who it was that was making this noise.

"Gorillas," he replied.

So I said, "Pitch a tent here. I like this location. We are going to hunt gorillas tomorrow."

But I fell ill that night, and going for a hunt the next day was out of the question. I had a fever for five days and became so weak from fasting that I had to rest for another few days. A bizarre incident occurred about this time.

That day I was on a restricted diet, in a feeble condition. A collection of Rabindranath's poetry that I had brought along kept me occupied. I would flip its pages on the occasional long waits inside the tent, and at other times I would spend time sitting on the camp chair outdoors. I looked at the river and listened to the birds. This is how I spent my days. Just before sunset a herd of elephants went by near us, causing a ruckus as they went to the river. They did not even look at us. All of this had become somewhat more familiar by then. It was not just elephants; I came across lions playing close by during our trek that didn't pay us any mind either.

The evening grew darker, and the avian symphony eventually ended as well. I also heard a cheetah somewhere out there in the vast solitude. I rose slowly and returned to my tent. Just two pieces of roti and some water let me get through the night, since I was unable to stomach anything more substantial.

African monkeys and birds don't wait for a proper sunrise before they start their activities of the day. Their ruckus roused me even before dawn broke.

I was famished. I opted to make my own breakfast since the servants were still asleep. The first thing I noticed was that three cans of jelly were missing from my table. Then I saw that the four rotis I had not consumed the day before had also vanished. I grew irritated. Surely a thief or hungry coolie had entered my tent during the night. I summoned the chief immediately. After he listened to me, he gathered his people together. However, none of them took responsibility for the theft. I said to them in frustration, "If I ever find a thief in my tent again, I will shoot him."

That night it rained quite heavily. I love the sound of rain when I go to sleep. Outside, while the earth bathed in the rain, the ground became muddy, and the travel clothes got wet—but I was happily inside my tent, keeping warm and cozy in my bed. This wonderful sensation caused me to get drowsy, and the sound of raindrops eventually lulled me to sleep.

The next morning we discovered that the three tins of biscuit that had been on the table had also disappeared. I got irrationally annoyed. It is never a big deal if food gets stolen in the city. But in the forest, far away from civilization, where even gold can't get you biscuits, theft of food meant that we would have to fold up our hunting expedition a few days earlier than planned.

Exiting the tent, I spotted them as soon as I glanced down. Footprints were easily discernible in the ground that was still soggy from yesterday night's rain. Human footprints.

I called the chief yet again, informed him about the theft, and showed him the footprints. He gazed at them thoughtfully for a while. It is the coolies' job to roam the African forests and detect wild animals, so tracking creatures by their footprints is part of their profession. I waited for his expert opinion. He began crawling all over, examining the prints closely. I could sense amazement in his face as he went about it. The seriousness of his look deepened as he stood up.

"What is the matter?"

He sighed and shrugged.

"You do not know what these are, do you? I can tell you with absolute certainty these belong to a human. And it must be one of the coolies. The closest village is a good twenty miles away. A human being, as I am sure you will agree, cannot possibly make it this far in the dark through this perilous forest."

"Yes, bwana, I agree."

"So it must be one of our coolies who has stolen the food?"

He shook his head and replied: "No bwana, this is not one of us."

"What do you mean?"

"Even if I told you, you would not believe me."

"Why?"

"Because you would think I'm lying to you."

"Ok, tell me what you think. I will believe you."

"Bwana, the one who came to your tent last night was not a man."

"What?"

"Yes, indeed, bwana. These footprints belong to a woman. I have no doubts at all."

"What the hell is wrong with you? This forest is 20 miles away from the village. The forest is full of gorillas, elephants, buffaloes and tigers. A woman came all this way to steal from us at night?"

He said deliberately, "Well, I have thought of those things too. This, however, is not up for debate. These footprints belong to a woman."

I stood there transfixed. It seemed like the chief was about to depart. I warned him, "Do not speak of this with the others."

He smiled tiredly and said, "I wouldn't have even if you hadn't asked me not to. If I told them, they would believe there's witchcraft here. They would flee and abandon us."

I contemplated the chief's theory for a considerable amount of time, but came to the conclusion that it was just too fantastic to be true. The terrifying forests of Kivu, where there are no signs of human civilization, where even fully armed hunting parties such as ours tread carefully, where every step of the way brings new nightmares of mortal danger, there, in the middle of the night, a woman all by herself—this is a joke. He must have been mistaken.

I left on my own with a gun in the afternoon, to see if I could hunt a few birds nearby. At least I would have a proper dinner tonight. I started walking along the river looking for birds in the trees close by. The sunbeams lit up the flowing river water, and the joyful songs of countless birds floated on the gentle breeze. I enjoyed the tranquility of this scene so much that I no longer felt like taking a life. A large wild pigeon sat down on one of the branches in the distance, but I did not chase it. It is as if my heart said: "As much right as you have to live in this bright sunny day, so do they." After wandering about for a while, I began to head back towards the tent.

A glint of an object on the beach caught my eye. I approached it and discovered it was my tin of biscuits. I picked it up immediately. It was completely empty—and the beach was covered in human footprints. Whoever stole my tin did not return to human civilization in the middle of the rainy night. Rather, they sat here right on this beach and devoured all my biscuits. Who could it be? Even if it wasn't a coolie or a woman, what kind of a human was this? If a man, what sort of man? Does he have no place to shelter? Does he then not have the usual fears of humankind?

I was thinking these thoughts as I walked back. I noticed the chief sitting quietly under a tree, so I went up to him and told him about my discovery. He again shook his head dispiritedly. He was behaving oddly for sure. It is as if he possessed some secret that he did not want to divulge to me. I did not press him, either. He already had some strange notions in his head, so he might have blurted out something even more nonsensical. I only said: "Chief, we need to apprehend this thief. I intend to stay awake tonight and keep watch. Will you be able to stay up and alert?"

He replied: "Yes, I have decided that tonight I shall be keeping vigil from this tree."

I thanked him.

Right after supper that night, I tucked myself into bed and turned off the lights. I did not sleep. The moon shone brightly in the cloudless sky. The chief was keeping watch outside from his treetop perch, so he would be able to see the thief for sure. I lay inside the tent completely awake. We would have a good chance of nabbing the crook tonight.

The only thing that disrupted the quiet of the night was the constant chirping of crickets. Every now and then the loud trumpet of an elephant could be heard coming from afar too. An owl sometimes bleated outside the tent, as if calling out just to keep me awake.

So I stayed awake and alert. Even though I had shut my eyes, my mind's eye stayed open. Sleep came and flirted with me several times, but I refused to give in to it. I forced myself to stay awake by any means necessary.

Dawn broke, and there was no sign of the thief. The cacophony of morning birds taunted me. I walked out of the tent, annoyed. The chief stood close by, so I expressed my frustration to him: "It was a waste staying up all night. The mischief maker didn't even turn up."

He replied: "They came."

"Is that so?"

"Yes, bwana. They came to these bushes right here."

"That's impossible. These bushes are so dense no human can come through them, whether day or night."

"Bwana, what makes you think they are human?"

"Uff, have you started believing in witches too?"

"What I believe, well, Allah alone knows. But they came through these bushes. I heard their footsteps on the dry grass. I inspected the grounds just now. The earth is still soft from the rain. I saw footprints and handprints on the ground. They were coming crawling through the bushes. But their vision is far superior to ours, so they must have seen me sitting on the treetop. There's no way they would dare to come out from the bushes after that."

I stood still in my seething rage.

He continued: "But bwana, this is the day we are meant to start again. We need to pack up camp. I was wondering when we were going to get started?"

I stopped him, determined to have my way: "First I shall catch this thief. Then, and only then, will we budge from here. Chief, you pitch your tent next to mine today. Don't go up the tree tonight, just stay up in your own tent. I will do the same. I'll shout out when I need you."

He nodded in assent.

So another night of staying awake. The moon was blazing in the clear night sky, the feral bloodlust of nocturnal carnivores was keeping them awake, my eyes were wide open, and in the bushes the thief was awake. The river was awake too, its soft song entrancing all who heard it.

The chief had said: "Why do you think they are human?" Ridiculous! Was he starting to believe in superstitions too? But why should it come as a shock? He's African too. This Africa is the home of all superstitions. This place reeks of specters, witchcraft, sorcery. Man-eating monsters are not your run-of-the-mill beasts; rather, they are malevolent sorcerers posing as humans and preying on the innocent. Which is why there are fewer ghosts than exorcists in these parts!

I had stayed up all day yesterday and today, so I dozed off while thinking these thoughts. I wasn't aware that I'd fallen asleep; a noisy rustling jolted me awake. There was someone inside the tent. It was too dark for me to make out any details, but a skunk-like noxious stench had filled up the tent. This was not a human smell at all.

I stopped breathing and lay absolutely still. The creature was also absolutely still. Perhaps I had made some noise when I woke up startled, so it was now watching me with its sharp eyes. Perhaps it could even see in the dark. Five minutes passed like this. In this silence the breath of the wild creature in the dark began to assault my ears. And that stench! Intolerable!

The rustling sound began again. Someone was going through things on my table. They must have thought me asleep. I first determined where the creature was in relation to the table. Then, without any warning, I jumped up straight and tackled the creature in the dark. Two strong arms shoved me aside so sharply that I fell back onto my bed. By sheer good fortune, the object that came to rest in my grasp was my electric torch—which, together with my gun, are the two things I sleep with at night. I turned the light on the creature, and what I saw I'll never forget.

Thick, medusa-like clusters of black hair framed a ferocious, dark face. It had a female face, and it looked human, yet also not. Those eyes were not human; they were blazing red with hunger. And were those human teeth, or something more like the keen, cruel, brutal teeth of an animal?

It was dazzled by the sudden glare of the torch. I quickly yelled, "Chief! Chief!"

The next moment, my tent was flooded with an ear-splitting, furious roar, the likes of which no human is capable of producing!

I shivered and reached for my rifle, and the creature bolted out of my tent. I heard piercing screams coming from the outside! It was the chief, screaming in pain! I rushed out from the tent and saw the man down on the ground, crumpled and crying, and the pitch-dark naked creature standing over him, its bare hands holding the man's neck in a death grip. In a word: brutal!

I could not risk shooting the chief when the two were so connected, so I brought the full force of my rifle butt down on the creature. It howled in anguish, half stood up and lunged at me like a viper, its wild hair lashing out in all directions. My rearward leap caused the creature to fall flat on the ground. It remained motionless where it had fallen.

I ran to the chief, who sat up without my help. I said: "Chief, you're bleeding from your neck!"

He pressed the area with a piece of cloth and said, "She wasn't able to go deep, but had you been a few minutes late I would be dead . . . but, what is that noise!" His eyes widened in the dark as he fearfully looked about.

True—it was as if the whole forest had suddenly woken up. The ground was rumbling and shaking, the trees were crumpling and breaking, and the bamboo forests were swaying and cracking. And with it an unknown, strange, and terrifying roar coming towards us!

By this point, most of the coolies had woken up and joined us. A full moon illuminated the sky, and the river burbled gently close to the majestic shadows of the forest. The moonlight had spread out across the earth like a soft, ethereal blanket. This tranquility was abruptly shattered by the advancing, deafening noise of a group of creatures marching towards us. We all froze in place and stared into the night forest—waiting for something to happen. The chief sprang to his feet and stood next to me. A look of terror had spread over his face; his eyes were popping in fear.

The alarmed birds arose noisily from the forests in the east, and a few monkeys and even a cheetah sprinted away westwards. The chief spoke in a quiver: "Bwana, right there! They are coming from over there!"

My throat was completely dry. "Who are they? Who is coming?"

But he said nothing more. His face was pale as death.

That terrible, indescribable sound was now close to us. It felt like an earthquake had struck. Never before had I heard such otherworldly sounds. These earth-shattering sounds were not human, but I knew of no other creature that could make them either. All of a sudden, the eastern bamboo grove fell apart, and then—oh, what is that! Who are they? I looked out into the moonlight and saw a dark barrier materializing in front of us. I just stood there, transfixed, staring at it. It seemed as though dozens of massive human arms were forming a wall!

A black thing sped past us, heading directly into that dark, living wall of arms. Glancing quickly around, I saw that the female creature had disappeared. We'd had no clue when she'd regained consciousness—we hadn't had time to check! Moments later, the figure had vanished into the wall's darkness. Excitement, terror, and awe had driven me to the brink of insanity, so I started to empty my rifle by firing at the wall of creatures. Having fallen asleep while wearing my bandolier, I continually reloaded and fired my rifle.

The chief stopped me and said, "Bwana, why are you wasting your bullets like this?"

I came to my senses. The daze cleared, and I saw that dark wall was no longer there. There was no longer any unearthly noise permeating the air, and the bamboo grove was similarly silent.

I let out a sigh and sat down on the ground. I inquired, exhausted, "What was that?"

"Gorillas."

"Gorillas? What did they want here?"

"To take back Tana."

"Who in the blazes is Tana?"

"The one who was stealing from your tent."

"Have you lost your mind, Chief? For the life of me, I cannot figure out what you are saying."

"Tana is a human female, bwana. The gorillas kidnapped her when she was a year old—that was fifteen years ago. She has been living with the gorillas since then. Even though she is human she lives and acts like a gorilla. I had heard this tale a long while ago, but this was the first time I've seen her. Allah forbid that I ever have to see her again."

In the glow of the moon, the forest took on the appearance of a fairy world. Tana, a human female, but humans are now her enemy. Perhaps her gorilla family is tenderly petting her injured head right now. I kept staring into that dark forest stupefied in wonder. What an alien land this is!

3 In the Lion's Den

I'd arrived in Uganda. A lion, wounded by me, had fled, leaving behind a trail of blood. I followed that trail deep into the forest. I had with me a few local coolies.

There was a massive mountain straight in front of us. The flat, level route that led to it ascended precipitously and disappeared into the mountain. The trail clearly indicated that the lion took this path.

I was getting ready to go up when the coolies' chief cautioned me: "Bwana, don't follow this path."

"Why?"

"This is the Juju[7] Mountain."

Incredulous, I said: "Juju Mountain? What is that?"

His expression hardened and he said: "There is no end to this mountain. I have never climbed it or been inside, but I have been told the people that reside there are not human. . . ."

"How is that a surprise? This is a forest, one shouldn't expect humans here anyway."

"No, bwana, that is not at all what I am saying. Inside that cursed place is the kingdom of the Jujus. The mere sight of them can make humans die of fright."

"I don't believe in Jujus, Chief. This is all crazy talk. I am heading up. Come with me."

Frightened, the chief shrieked: "Me? No way! I do not want to die this young. None of us will go up that mountain. You can ask for yourself if you like!"

I didn't even have to ask. The others said in unison: "Never!"

This was a setback. I'd shot an unusually large lion, and wounded it severely. I doubted it would be able to go much further. Should I let go of such a precious prize? No, whatever lay ahead, I intended to continue the hunt. So I told the others, "You all wait here. I will go up by myself and return with the lion."

The chief urged me again: "Please listen to me, bwana. No one who goes up that mountain returns to tell the tale."

I laughed at these superstitions of the uncivilized. There was no point in continuing the debate. I just picked up the trail and started going up the steep mountain cautiously. Every hunter knows that an injured lion or tiger can be extremely dangerous. As a result, I was on the lookout and ready to use my weapon. Roughly three hundred feet higher up, the path took an abrupt right turn into dense woods. It was so thick that standing upright seemed quite impossible. But I was possessed by the hunter's bloodlust, so I started crawling along the trail without hesitation. The remoteness of the forest made it obvious that no human had set foot there before. There was no sign of life—even the sun refused to shine here.

Suddenly the path came to an end. In front of me was a cave, and the trail led within it. Perhaps this was the lion's den?

It was pitch dark inside. I was unable to see a thing even after trying to let my eyes adapt. As far as I could make out, there was no lion here. Perhaps it was lying in wait inside, watching me. Perhaps it would pounce at me without warning and unleash its fury. I had my electric torch with me, so I switched it on and looked into the cave. I saw the lion at once. It just lay there on the ground about five feet away. Even when I shone the light directly on it there was no movement at all. It wasn't breathing; I had killed it. However, the situation still warranted caution. Injured beasts can often play dead, and then the moment the hunter comes close they will spring to life and strike a fatal blow. I kept the torch lit and fired a few more rounds into its body. When it still didn't move, I went inside the cave. I was ecstatic that my efforts had borne fruit.

The cave was small, but oh, how frightful it was. Darkness seeped into the black rock all around. The floor of the cave was covered in white bones that had been stripped of all their flesh. Perhaps human bones lay amongst them too?

Something caught my eye as soon as I had that notion. A piece of fabric was caught in a pile of bones. I prodded it with my rifle. It was a coat! So this lion was used to eating humans too. Something dropped out of the coat at my prodding, and I crouched down to pick it up. It was a small diary, the journal of the unfortunate soul who'd lost his life to this lion. It must have belonged to some white explorer. Curious to identify this man, I opened the diary and shone my torch on it.

With a shock, I realized that the writing was Bangla! I was astonished to see traces of Bangla in this remote lion-cave in Uganda. An introspective Bengali had traveled all the way here just to be dinner for this cruel lion.

But I shouldn't have been so surprised. After all, I am a Bengali too, and this lion could easily have made a meal of me. Then my remains too would lie on the pile of bones like those of this unfortunate man. No one would ever have found either of us again.

I came out of the cave—that gruesome pit of savagery—to the open air outside. I remembered my servants at once—I had forgotten all about them in my frenzied pursuit of game. They'd named this Juju Mountain. Why did they name it so? Why did people die here? Nobody within miles ever approached this peak. Why?

I looked around carefully for answers to that "why." But I found nothing suspicious. A barren mountain, a bleak mountain road, a forlorn forest. The stillness and the quiet slowly merging into the pale pink evening light. It did seem peculiar, but nothing really frightening to me. But it would soon be evening, so it would be a mistake to loiter here much longer. I rapidly went down the mountain.

The expression on the chief's face said it all. He had not expected me to return.

I could not help but chuckle. I asked the chief, "Why is your jaw hanging open like that? Do not be afraid, I am not a ghost."

In a trembling whisper, the chief asked, "Did you see them?"

"Who?"

"The Ones Who Are Not Human?"

"Yes, I did see a creature that was not human."

He turned white in terror and began to shiver. I burst out laughing and said, "Indeed! I saw such a creature! And that was none other than our injured lion. It's lying in a cave up above, dead as a doornail."

The chief spoke in disbelief: "You saw nothing else at all, bwana?"

"Nope. Not a thing. Not even a jungle rat."

The chief sighed in relief: "You are a fortunate man. Those who climb this mountain never come down again."

I asked him bluntly: "Tell me, did a Bengali ever go up this mountain?"

He replied, "Yes indeed, bwana, precisely one year ago. I brought him here too. Just like you, he would not listen to me. I warned him many times, but he went right up. He never returned."

"Well, how could he? He was eaten by a lion. I found his bones in the lion's den."

But the man refused to accept that the Bengali had died at the hands of a lion. He kept repeating 'Devil,' 'Juju,' and other such things. I refused to entertain any further superstitious nonsense.

The diary was still in my possession. I decided I would make it a priority to get to know my fellow Bengali as soon as I returned to camp. What an unlucky soul! No doubt his family was unaware of his tragic end.

4 The Eyes in the Barrel

After dinner I stretched out on my camp-cot and began to read the diary. The more I read his account, the more marvelous it seemed. This was a strange, wondrous, inhuman history or autobiography: If you start reading this diary you will not be able to put it down. A narrative as incredible as this is one I have never heard before, and am unlikely to ever hear again. If anybody back in the city had told me this tale, I would not have believed them. If someone had insisted to me that this was the truth, I would have had them committed to a mental institution.

But here, in the deep forests of Africa . . . Everything seems possible here. I lifted the door of the tent and looked outside.

Such a pristine night. The sky spread out like an ocean and the wind was made of cascading moonbeams. There stood the Juju Mountain, its summit adorned with a silver crown above the shadowy clouds, its slopes covered in lush, impenetrable forest that no man would dare enter. Yet in the moonlight even this bone-chilling forest seems utterly glorious. I could hear the ceaseless nighttime music of the forest. The roars of ravenous lions that shook the forest floor could be heard from near and far. Fearful herds of zebras galloped away in the dark. The incessant, manic laughs of the hyenas. A troop of monkeys swinging through the treetops. The last shrieks of a bird trapped in a snake's maw warning other birds to take flight. A cobra's hiss announcing that it, too, belongs in this endless struggle for life. The owls hooting away as if to poison the night. And beneath all this, like the hungry growls of a stomach, a steady, eternal, forest hum. The many sounds of forest life, mixed with the sounds of this deathless hum, create a bizarre soundscape.

The local attendants and coolies were gathered around a fire pit just ahead. In the glare of the flames, their features seemed bloodied. Even though I did not speak their language and could not understand a word they were saying, I was able to pick out the three-word phrase: "Juju! Juju! Juju!"

They must have been discussing the Juju Mountain still. These are simple, uncivilized folk—their minds unencumbered by the complexity and concerns of urban life. Whenever a bizarre new idea comes to them, it remains with them forever. Still, was it only superstition that explained their fear of Juju Mountain's interior? After reading the Bengali hunter's diary, I had more doubts than previously, and could no longer ignore their concerns. Unlike them, the diarist must have been a civilized individual. The writing style suggests that he was well-educated. It did not seem as though he was merely narrating a bad dream. However, the story he told . . .

The chief suddenly appeared before me in the tent. He was clearly afraid and agitated.

I asked: "What's the matter, Chief?"

He said: "Are you planning to hunt here any longer?"

I replied: "Yes. Big game seems to be easy to get here. I think I might stay here for a fortnight."

He responded: "OK, in that case, we'll take our leave. It is imperative that we get out of here immediately."

"What! Why?"

"Men shouldn't linger in these places. The Jujus have cast a curse on all the rocks and stones in this area."

I laughed: "Uff, this again, Chief?"

He shot back: "It's not madness, bwana. We saw something just now."

My curiosity was piqued: "You saw something now? Juju? Ghost? Witch? Monster?"

He was serious: "No, bwana, none of that. One shouldn't laugh about such things. It is inappropriate to make light of such situations. If I ever see something like what I witnessed today again, I will not be around to tell the story."

My impatience was growing as I demanded, "What did you see?"

"We've always assumed, sir, that the Jujus remain within the mountain. They'd never before revealed themselves outside it. So we'd gone about our business, around the camp, without any anxiety. It wasn't until today that I learned they could descend the mountain. There is no way this did not start with you. You disregarded our advice. You, a mere human, chose to contaminate their holy place. They must have descended from the mountain to exact vengeance."

I'd been lying down on the cot talking to him, but now I sat up and yelled: "OK, Chief. Either tell me what you saw right away, or just leave the tent. I don't have time for your nonsense."

"I had gone to the river to fetch water," he said. "When I was returning I saw something roll away hastily in front of me and disappear into the forest. I saw it clearly in the moonlight."

"So what was it? An animal?"

"No."

"Nor a human?"

"No. Just a small barrel."

I said, haltingly: "A small . . . barrel?"

"Yes, bwana. A small barrel. Whoever has seen a barrel come to life and roll about?"

"Perhaps someone was just trying to scare you by rolling a barrel."

"No, bwana. I promise you, there was no one else there. And there's something else. I swear that I saw two fiery eyes peering out from inside that barrel, glaring at me as it rolled along. I dropped my bucket and raced back to camp. We have to leave this cursed place immediately. Tomorrow." Having said this, he exited the tent.

I could not dismiss the chief's words any longer. If he was lying to me, then the man who'd written the diary had been lying as well. I had suspected embellishment in the man's account in many places, as if I was reading some fairytale or an amusing children's story, but it was not possible to wholly disbelieve the account anymore. Perhaps it was overblown in parts; after all, no man can resist the temptation in telling a good tale. Still, I am a modern twentieth-century man, a college-educated, motorcar-driving, scientifically minded man. Why should I take at face value whatever claims this uncivilized man and this unknown dead adventurer make? Who knows, maybe the man who wrote this diary had suffered a mental breakdown? Or perhaps he was writing a fantastic voyage like *Gulliver's Travels*? I would have asked him to explain, but death had silenced him eternally. There was no way to communicate with him from the beyond.

Suddenly, I had an idea: Maybe I could verify what the chief had told me. The chief's tall tale and the diary did have points of agreement between them. How was that possible? If the chief was telling the truth, then the story in the diary surely was true. I shouldn't let go of a chance to verify such a fabulous discovery.

I got up at once with urgency and donned my full hunting gear. Fear crept up on me, but I forced it out of my mind. Why should one who has left the lush vegetation of Bengal for the bleak darkness of the African jungles to battle its lions, elephants, and rhinos, and who carries an ammo-filled pistol, a revolver, and a hunting knife, shrink from confronting danger? Thanks to our capacity to voluntarily immerse ourselves in situations fraught with extreme peril, humans have risen to the position of the planet's most successful animal species. How did we learn that there is a North Pole and a South Pole, how did we discover the North American continent, how did we invent aircraft and submarines? It was the thrill of the unknown! To make such discoveries, many have joyfully risked fates worse than death. The thrill of danger is at the root of all new discoveries. Those who seek danger, theirs is the earth. Theirs is the sky.

I put on my gear in this frame of mind. I tucked a torch into my belt, and I also made sure to carry a bright, long-burning petrol lantern. In the half-darkness even the slightest movement of trees could induce hallucinations. But all illusions would be dispelled by the stark, calm flame.

Outside my tent I discovered that the coolies and the servants had begun to strike camp. Addressing the Chief, I asked, "What is going on here?"

"They are genuinely afraid. Many of them are getting ready to leave this evening and are frantically packing their bags. But where are you off to?"

"To the river."

"What! Why, bwana?"

"To verify your story."

He couldn't believe his ears. After a pause, he said: "Please, bwana. Don't do this. The curse of the Jujus is all over that place. No one who ventures there will return alive. If you go there by yourself you will surely die."

"Why would I go alone? You will show me the way—you have nothing to fear."

"Me? Is that a joke, bwana?" he sputtered. "I am not crazy! I have a wife and kid at home, I am not suicidal!"

"All right, just show me the way to the river. I will go there by myself."

He pointed. "There, the place is straight down that way. It is quite close. But sir, please, listen to me, do not confront the Jujus."

I went on my way. It would have been futile to argue with him.

I have previously mentioned how bright the night was. Luminosity pervaded every surface. Before me, the path to the river coiled like a motionless python. The moonlight cast a magical glow on the woods on each side of the road. It seemed as though Juju Mountain was rubbing up against the clear sky.

The forest seemed isolated but not uninhabited. The mysterious forest sounds came from every side—the hyena's mad laugh, the terrified screams of the monkeys, the hooting owl—and so many other inexplicable sounds. The only thing missing was the ear-shattering roar of the lion, a familiar sound of these parts of the African jungle. Rather than a cause for celebration, this was alarming. All experienced hunters in Africa know that one should be extra careful when the lions are quiet. They are silent only when they spot a prey, waiting to strike quietly like a thief. Who knows, maybe the king of beasts was looking at me right now with its greedy bloodthirsty eyes.

Lantern in hand, I cautiously made my way to the water. I wasn't worried about the lions. I was only thinking of the words of the chief and the diarist: Juju and the living barrel!

Something resembling a cheetah sprinted through the woods. A few baboons peeked out of the bushes and bared their teeth at me. They did not expect to see a human walking here at night.

A pack of birds suddenly flew out of the forest with agitated chirps. Every hunter knows the meaning of this: the birds must have caught sight of some fierce predator nearby. As I looked in their direction, the trees swayed and stopped moving, as if an invisible animal had suddenly come to a halt. I did the same and waited silently. There was no motion at all for quite a while. So I started walking again. I felt uneasy passing along that trail.

The mountain and lakes were still and peaceful under the moonlight, and the sky was adorned with the moon like a diamond. There was no dearth of flowers here either. I've read in magazines that poets find such places very romantic. But if I were to abandon a poet here and say, "Come, write a poem about this! Everything you love is right here—the rising moon, the blooming flower, the perfumed crisp breeze!" I want to know whether they would write poetry, pass out, or flee like the wind!

I made my way to the riverbank, where I spied nothing unusual. Whatever one might fear in a forest is here, true, but those are the things that the hunter is looking for! But what I came here to see, the things described on every page of the diary, the thing that gave the Chief the willies, of these there is no trace whatsoever. I laughed and thought to myself, "Fantastic creatures are the stuff of fairytales and children's stories. I feel stupid to have come out here all kitted out in the middle of the night, when I should have just been sleeping after a hard day's work."

I surveyed the river again. A crocodile was lying there looking at me. "My friend!" said its eyes. "Why don't you come just a little bit closer! I will show you what I do when I am hungry."

A bloat of hippos floated in the middle of the river. A few calves were playing in the water, some bumping into their mothers, others splashing about.

Suddenly I sensed that there were more eyes on me than those of the hippos and the crocodile. I was surrounded by a pack of unseen beings. At first glance, the trail seemed deserted, and the surrounding forest appeared completely still. Yet this eerie feeling of being observed disturbed me. This hadn't been the case a few moments earlier. Was there a lion? A tiger? What was hiding in the bushes?

It's not shocking that a wild creature would stay out of sight. It is possible that whatever had come this way was simply hiding out because of me, even if it had come here to get a sip of water. Maybe it was lying in wait to see whether it wanted to snack on me before getting a drink.

Whatever you may feel reading this right now, I didn't feel good at all at that moment. I put the lantern down. I took out the torch and shone it on the trees on either side of the trail. And then . . .

I saw it!

What were those two eyes? Through the bushes two fiery red orbs were peering at me! Two furious and fiercely hungry burning eyes! Was it a lion? A tiger? Whatever it might be, I immediately unshouldered my rifle and fired two rounds into the grass.

The next thing I knew, the sky was filled with a scream of unimaginable horror! No lion or tiger could ever make such a terrible cry! Something went running away—could it be a barrel? The whole forest was suddenly filled with shrill, horrible cries, enough to make even the most courageous hunter run for cover. No human has ever heard anything like that. I stood there uncertain of what to do next. All I was thinking was: "What monster is this that can utter such unearthly screams?" But what happened next made me lose my nerve altogether.

I had positioned myself smack-dab in the middle of the path. About ten to twelve feet away was where the forest began. Any monster intent on attacking me would have to cover at least that distance. But out of nowhere a snake-like thing shot from within the trees and struck my left hand. As my rifle clattered to the ground, the tentacle caught my hand with an iron grip and started to drag me into the woods.

I was momentarily too stunned to attempt to release myself. I was on the verge of being dragged off the trail when I realized that my right hand was still free. I quickly took out my revolver and fired several rounds in the direction of my assailant. The grip suddenly relaxed.

Although I hadn't caught a clear glimpse of what had gripped me and then let me go, it had managed to drag me nearly a dozen feet. I was dizzy with fear. I didn't dare to experiment any further—I sprinted back towards my tent. The inhuman screams pursued me along my run.

No doubt believing that I was being followed when they saw me sprint into the camp, the coolies screamed and fled, never to be seen again. I cannot blame them for cowardice. Perhaps they too had seen or heard of such things that I'd only now seen with my own eyes. Only my maker and I know how I endured that night of terror, worry, and sleeplessness. I left the cursed place the very next morning. My expensive rifle and lantern I abandoned. Even in the light of day I didn't feel safe going back for them. It is true that peril reveals a man's true nature, but even so surely there is a limit to how much one man can accept. No matter how much you may like seeking thrills, it is foolish to leap into a river without knowing how to swim.

The rest of this book I will devote to transcribing the contents of the Bengali's diary. Whether you think it is to be believed or not is up to you. The author of the diary has written of his adventures in clear and understandable language. I have not excised a single line from his account. In order to include it within my narrative, I have only added a few chapter headings.

5 The Diary Begins

There is no doubt about it—the coolies were telling the truth.

I have seen with my own eyes the possibility of the impossible! If I did not have nerves of steel, I would have gone insane.

Sometimes I have to pinch myself to be sure I am not in some kind of outlandish dream. But then I look at the sketches which I carried with me from that strange land. The sketches, at least, do not appear to be part of a dream.

My tale will be recorded as quickly as possible. I am in a dire state of health, so bad I cannot even begin to describe it. It has been seven days since I last ate, and three since I last drank anything. The climate on this side of the mountain is dry as a desert. I cannot muster the energy to go on.

Although the beginning of my tale will undoubtedly shock you, I think you will find that, by its conclusion, horror has given way to riotous hilarity. Many of you may even see my situation as farcical. However, human existence itself is a farce; the grin of one individual may be lethal to another. If you find my story humorous, please remember that throughout my ordeal, humor was the last thing on my mind.

This story might be called "The History of a Nightmare." When a person wakes up, the terrifying dream they had while sleeping now seems like a joke. That is almost how I feel, but I am close to the end of my life. I won't live long enough to see the humor in this situation—more's the pity.

I am now hiding out in a cave high in the mountains, attempting to complete this diary. My expectations for living much longer or seeing another human are low. But I hope that my journal will be found by someone in the future—and that these lines will be read by human eyes.

*

None of the coolies would agree to come with me. They said, in unison: "No one goes to the Juju Mountain."

This infuriated me. Determined to solve the mystery of the Juju Mountain before I left Africa, I left the coolies in the camp and began my ascent.

I climbed, and climbed, and climbed. Although I did not see any Juju creature, I can attest to this mountain's bleakness. There is no sign of human life—or any other kind—here. Things began to feel scarier the higher I ascended. Why did humans avoid this place? Why were there no signs of habitation? This mountain should be a poet's paradise, a pilgrimage for the devout! It was stunningly beautiful in the sunlight, with magnificent waterfalls singing melodious songs in their own language as they rolled down to the ground. It was covered in wild, colorful flowers and bushes, and there was lush green grass covering the ground all the way to the volcano. So why did humans stay away? Why had these mountains never been described in any guidebook?

As I continued to ascend, I was overcome by another, even more eerie sensation: I sensed that creatures were following me on both sides of the trail. Although no people or animals dwelled here, I was not entirely alone. Things were cautiously watching me. I double-checked the trail ahead of and behind me, and I peeked into the bushes, but I didn't see anything. Still, these invisible spirits stalked me relentlessly. I couldn't shake the sensation. Uff, I felt so uneasy!

After four hours of climbing, something caught my eye. A narrow path had been carved out of the mountain's side; in places, it was caked in dried mud. Inspecting this path for human footprints, I instead discovered strange skidmarks. It appeared as though someone had dragged cylindrical objects along this path when the ground was wet. But whoever had dragged these cylinders hadn't left any footprints—how?

I had been standing at the edge of a crevice, while I was pondering over these mysteries. Suddenly I slipped and fell. I hurtled into the crevice as though I were plunging into hell. My body shattered and cracked as I dropped into the darkness, and I screamed in agony.

Suddenly I hit a rock, and lost consciousness.

6 Sixteen Arms Long

I felt myself lying on a table when I recovered consciousness. I discovered only later that it was an operating table, or more precisely, a table used to alter people.

It took me several moments to realize that I was not lying on the table, but rather that the table was resting on my back. The table was suspended from the ceiling, and I was beneath it, looking straight down at the center of the room. I was not restrained in any way, but I did not fall. Though subsequently I would learn the scientific reason for all of this, in that moment my body froze, and I imagined I was having a nightmare.

Suddenly, I observed a little barrel on the ground with two eyes staring at me from within. This comical face resembled a child's drawing of a round moon with two eyes, a nose, a mustache, and a mouth. Again, I felt certain that this was all a dream.

The moon-face smiled. "Ah, you are finally awake. Amal, do you believe this is all a dream?"

I blurted out: "What do you mean—it isn't a dream?"

"No."

"So where am I? All I remember is tumbling down the hillside."

"Exactly. We picked you up from where you fell. Had we had not come to your rescue, you would undoubtedly have perished. Both your legs and your spine were broken in the fall. In the end, it was my scientific knowledge that saved your life."

The moon-face was confusing me. I no longer thought it was just a dream, but what could it be? Can a human hang from the ceiling without any support? And this moon-face that was staring and talking to me, has anyone ever seen such a face? My head began to spin.

The face in the barrel said: "Amal, you have been cured."

I asked: "How do you know my name?"

"We read your journal. Hold on, let me lower you . . ." As he said this, he did something that made the table—along with me—slowly rotate and descend to the floor.

The moon-face said, "Now you may get down from the table."

I slowly sat upright, then stepped down from the operating table.

A hand shot out from the barrel holding a glass. The moon-face said: "Here, drink this."

There was something green in the glass. As soon as I drank it, I felt a kind of sharp and painful lightning shoot through me.

I said, fearfully: "What did you make me drink?"

"There's nothing to worry about," the moon-face replied with a laugh. "It will help you."

I asked again: "So where am I?"

"Within the borders of a secret African nation."

"How did you learn Bangla?"

"Everyone here speaks Bangla. But I will explain our past later. For now, please pay attention to what I am saying. I know you are a Bengali. However, outsiders are prohibited from entering this realm. I brought you here because I want to do some experiments on you. But I don't know if the king will let you remain here. The court will assemble soon enough. You will have to wait to find out whether you are allowed to remain or if you are going to be put to death."

I shrieked: "Put to death?"

The moon-face replied, quite calmly: "Yes, indeed. That is our law, after all, for all outsiders who come here."

Such a perfectly ghastly law. I felt my stomach churn.

The moon-face spoke reassuringly: "But don't worry your head about this for now, Amal. I will try my best to see you aren't executed."

"Thank you," I replied, gratefully. "But may I know your name?"

The moon-face said: "No one calls me by my name in this place. Just call me Science Master. As the king's minister of knowledge I am responsible for all matters pertaining to science and learning." Saying this, the Science Master began to pace back and forth in the room.

The creature's movements threw me into a panic. I noticed that three legs had shot out of the barrel, from which still peered the Science Master's face. This barrel of legs and face was scuttling all around me.

I had once read of a magic kettle in a Japanese fairytale. That kettle had an awful habit—sometimes it would shoot out legs and grow a face, and would show off its dancing skills. But that was a children's fable, meant as amusement. What I had in front of me at that moment was a barrel that was completely alive and moving all around me. This was not something I could dismiss as an opium eater's dream.[8]

Seeing my gaping expression, the Science Master grinned: "So you believe my physique seems somewhat new and different? I promise to explain it as soon as I can, but right now I have to go to work. My daughter will soon be here—you may talk to her while I am gone."

Do you know what a paper snake looks like? It is little when coiled up, but if you blow into it, it stretches out as long as your arm. As quickly as that, a hand shot out from the barrel, opened the door, then shot back into the barrel. But the door must have been at least 16 or 17 arm's lengths away from the Science Master's barrel! The next instant, I saw the three legs coiling back into the barrel, after which the barrel rolled across the floor and through the door.

I could hardly believe my eyes. Are such things even possible?

I was standing there dumbfounded and perspiring from worried thoughts when I saw that a fresh, lovely figure had entered the room.

7 The Kind Kamala

There was no reason to fear the vision that walked in. Your eyes would have teared up in delight and your heart would have felt lighter and happier at the sight. She was beautiful, like a princess from a fairytale.

I have read about such creatures before in folk tales, in epics, in stories and novels. But this girl, oh! She was more gorgeous than words could ever express. It is difficult to conceive of a more stunning skin color, figure, or face! In this godless, otherworldly barrel-kingdom, the sight of my host's daughter cast a spell on me.

She drew closer and greeted me with a warm smile: "You must be my father's guest. Would you mind telling your name?"

"Amalkumar Sen."

"I assume you must be quite terrified?"

"Is there a human soul that wouldn't feel scared in this place? Did you notice who or what it was that just exited the room?"

She giggled and said: "Of course, why would I not?"

"And you still wonder why I am scared? How many other moon-faces have you trapped in barrels?"

"There are far too many to count."

"What the—what do you mean? What do you do with them?"

"What should we do? Some are my friends, some are my foes, some are people I play with. And then there is my father—"

"Your father? That creature—moon-faced, arms sixteen arms long, a barrel body, three legs? That's your father?"

"He is indeed."

"But you seem to be no different than us humans . . ."

"Yes, but this is not my true form."

I asked, stupefied: "What do you mean?"

"I am merely imitating the form of my ancestors. I do not much like my true form."

Was she out of her mind? What could it mean to have a 'true' form—or an 'untrue' form?

She continued: "My true form resembles my dad's, though he has a mustache and I don't. I am as pliable as he is, oftentimes, because we cannot maintain the illusion of a stable form for long. It's painful."

I could not believe my ears. Pliable like her father, imitating her ancestors' "stable" form . . . all this was making my head spin. Was she kidding me? If she was attempting to play a cruel prank, her innocent, childish countenance belied any malice. Did that mean I really was in a spirit kingdom? Many believe that male and female spirits roam in dimensions beyond our own. Could it be I was in such a place—and that I would have to embrace the horrible possibility that I'd perished a long time ago on that Juju mountain, and had become a spirit? Maybe like the famous Alice I was roaming in a wonderland, trapped in my own unconscious. But I refrained from expressing these distressing thoughts. I asked instead: "So you live in a barrel?"

"Yeah. Like tortoises in their shell, we make ourselves at home in barrels. As we don't have bones in our bodies, we can assume whatever form we like. Our bodies are like rubber, all of us can stretch or compress them to whatever size we choose. Look at this—" the girl said, as she began to stretch out her neck—so high and so thin that her head disappeared through an open window!

I screamed in horror: "Stop it! Stop it now! This is too much for me—I can't breathe . . ."

Instantaneously her head returned to her shoulders, like a rubber ball bouncing back. She was amused. "Look, we can perform all of these things with our eyes as well." Saying that, she popped her eyeballs six inches from their sockets, then popped them back in!

I was utterly terrified. My heart beat so rapidly I thought it would explode. I'd heard about shapeshifting monsters and she-monsters in fairy tales . . . was I in a land of monsters? Every hair on my body, from head to toe, stood on end. I knew this was real, it wasn't a dream—but what was this bizarre, fantastical world?

"Please, girl, don't frighten me anymore," I begged. "It would be kinder if you'd just kill me."

She giggled again: "Ha ha—fine. I see that all this scares you. I apologize, and I won't do it any more. But really, there is nothing to be alarmed about. You will get used to everything in two days. OK, now I should go." With that, she left.

I was annoyed by how disrespectful the young woman was. She'd begun by addressing me formally, but by the time she'd left she was using quite familiar terms. By tomorrow, would she dare to address me by my first name —like a friend?

I suddenly noticed that the Science Master had quietly slipped back into the room. He was standing on his three legs near the door and smirking.

"Ha! Why are you standing so rigidly?" he asked. "Did Kamala frighten you with her antics? She cannot help it. Did you like her initial appearance? Of course you did. To you those kinds of faces are attractive—though we do not think so. Are you curious why? OK, let me tell you a little bit about us."

8 The History of the Juju Kingdom

The Science Master began: "You must have heard about Vijay Singh of Bengal, who sailed to Sinhala by water and reigned there for many years?[9] A group of his followers—whose ship was separated from Vijay's fleet by a terrible storm—were our forebears. After many years of drifting at sea, the ship ended up landing here in Africa.

"The ship's captain was a man called Chandrasen.[10] The term "brave warrior" alone does not do justice to his character. He had extensive knowledge of several shastras[11] and arcana. Most of his time was devoted to researching scientific secrets. Well-versed in areas unknown to even the brightest minds of your scientists today, he discovered a technique to improve people physically and spiritually to the point of perfection. Even if I took the time to explain this to you, you still would not get it. If you're interested, maybe I'll show you our children's science museum.

"Chandrasen began by experimenting on his shipmates. We are the result of that experiment!

"In the past, as I've explained, we were no different from you primitive Bengalis. We used to be weak, worthless, and imperfect beings just like you, but that has all changed. Our souls are now the masters of our bodies, not their slaves. We do not have skeletons, since there is no use in having bones. We can mold our bodies into any form whatsoever, as Kamala has demonstrated to you. Our brains are not confined to the jail of our skulls—instead, they are manifested throughout our bodies, which is why we have limitless control of every organ and appendage.

"Have a look at how I can manipulate my own appearance." (Saying this, the Science Master began to transform his face in so many different ways that my body froze in terror.) "It's entirely up to us how many or few hands and legs we have." (He extruded some twenty arms and legs from his barrel and began to move them around). "We can stroll along as slowly as you do, or we can run faster than your motorcars. I also get to decide how long I want to live.

"Lanka, or Sinhala, was formerly home to King Ravana.[12] His body had twenty limbs and ten heads. He could also disguise himself as a regular person if he so desired. Kumbhakarna, his elder sibling, towered above even the tallest palm trees. Such feats demonstrate the power of the spirit over the material form. You are all ordinary humans, so you write this legend off as the ramblings of a cannabis-smoker. But this is why you are so stupid. Could you really believe that the authors of the great epics *Ramayana* and *Mahabharata* were stoned?

"It is quite likely that Chandrasen learnt the secret techniques to completely alter human bodies because he had traveled to the land of King Ravana. Perhaps scientists experimenting with these secret techniques showed him their methods. Now we are the last people on Earth with this knowledge. If you remain for a while, perhaps you will learn a few new things, too.

"OK, that is everything for today, Amal. To keep filling your little brain with fresh knowledge would cause it to explode. Come with me."

I followed him into the next room, where an abundance of fresh produce was piled high on two small tables. The Science Master crossed his three legs under himself and sat down at one table, motioning for me to do the same. "Sit down, Amal, sit. Let's eat. We don't waste much time on food." He then stretched his mouth wide like a python and devoured an entire basket of fruit in under two minutes. He finished by drinking some water and said, "Done! Hope you have had enough. Let's get going."

Had enough? Maybe these people don't need to spend much time eating—if you can eat enough for ten people in two minutes, why would you need any time? I feared I would die of starvation if I continued dining with this moon-face. I was unable to eat even two apples in two minutes. So while the Science Master drank his water I pocketed a few fruits for snacking later.

"Overeating turns your head into mush," he murmured as he dried his face. "Therefore, we are only going through the motions of eating. However, there are still some fools in our world who believe that consuming more food would result in greater physical strength. I hope they get what they deserve for being so foolish. Oh, speak of the devil—one such is coming over to us."

I turned around to see a barrel-being come our way, rolling and panting. His barrel was so huge that two of the Science Master would easily fit inside it. His face was enormous and he was covered in warts the size of golf-balls. He had such a sanctimonious smile on his lips that it made my skin crawl. I took an instant dislike to him.

He came close and looked me up and down. "Dear Master," he said, "is this the unusual creature you mentioned? Huh. I came all this way to see it."

The Science Master introduced us: "The gentleman's name is Amalkumar Sen—he hails from Bengal. Bhombol, don't forget your manners. Show some courtesy."

Bhombol changed his tune immediately: "Of course, of course. Your friend is my friend too. By the way, where is Kamala?"

"She must have gone to the minister's house. But anyway, can you do something for me? Show Amal around a bit?"

"Of course, of course," Bhombol replied. "I would lay down my life for you, so this is but a small favor. Come, Amal-babu, let us go for a stroll. I can take you to the children's science museum. There's also a good hotel nearby, we can eat a bit too. What do you say?" He slapped me hard on my back in jest.

The Science Master ordered: "Bring him back by sundown. Remember, he is your responsibility now." He folded his limbs back into his barrel and sped out of the house.

Bhombol waggled his eyebrows: "I must do what the master commands. Amal-babu, so you are what they call a human? What do you think of us?" He flashed his teeth in a wide grin.

I did not reply.

He continued with a grin: "Can you roll like us?"

I was a bit annoyed. I said: "Of course not. It is obvious I do not have a barrel."

"There is no avoiding it then. I am doomed to use my legs to walk like an inferior human. It can be quite exhausting. But well, please come this way."

We exited the house via a walkway that sloped steeply downwards. These were apparently stairs, but they had no steps, as they were solely designed for rolling. I found it difficult to descend, and almost slipped and fell on my face twice. Ultimately, I was unable to maintain my equilibrium, and I slipped, tumbled down, and bruised myself.

Bhombol did not help me in the slightest. He casually rolled down and stopped next to me. Grinning broadly, he said: "See? There are so many perks to living in your own barrel."

I replied, resentfully: "You will see who has the last laugh if you visit our country. If you tried to climb down our stairs, your barrel would shatter completely."

He scoffed: "Who's going to your country? You are all so uncivilized!"

I kept silent. We walked till we reached the main Royal boulevard.

It was a bizarre sight. On both sides were rows of houses, but none of them looked alike, either in design or style! And all the roofs were arched, twisted, grotesque! There were skyscrapers here, too, like there are in the office district in Kolkata, but just the thought of using their rolling staircases made my heart skip a beat. Although someone with a dozen monster limbs may be able to scale them, I think I would be crushed to a pulp if I attempted any such thing.

The streets were tranquil and quiet, a far cry from the chaotic streets back home. There were barrels rolling all over the place, some fast, some slow. There were hardly any that were walking on their legs. Those who were on their feet, though, stood on three legs, which made me think that, though they can use more legs if needed, their usual style was to use just three legs.

A lot of wheels were whizzing by on the roads. The diameter of some of these wheels had to be at least eight or ten feet! They were going at the speed of a motorcar, and it was impressive to see how deftly they were able to weave in and around the moving barrels. But it also became clear that it didn't really matter if they did strike a barrel. I saw one wheel just roll atop a barrel, cross it, and continue rolling—without causing any problem at all for either party. Such 'accidents' must be so common here that this was not even worth their attention.

The big barrel next to me, which is to say Bhomboldas, licked his lips once and said: "So, Amala, I see that you are floored by our country, eh!"

I snapped: "Why do you call me Amala? My name is Amal."[13]

He bared his teeth again: "Why do you get offended with such jokes? Amal and Amala are identical."

I said: "No, they are in no way identical. I do not appreciate these jokes."

He replied: "Oh my god, you are such a humorless country dolt! You get so upset at something so trivial! Do you even realize how you look right now?" Saying this, he proceeded to contort his face in a weird manner, until before long his face was exactly like mine. Only those who have endured it can comprehend the nature of such a horrifying experience. Another "me" emerged in front of my eyes. I said in exasperation: "I give up! I apologize. Stop this, please."

His visage snapped back into his own nasty Bhombol face. He grinned: "Indra, the king of the gods, assumed the guise of the Rishi Goutam. I can replicate what he did because I know it all. And Science Master's daughter, Kamala, is likewise quite skilled in this art. No one in this whole kingdom is as competent in these arts as us. Anyway, we are wasting our time in idle chatter, and I am getting hungry. Let us visit the museum first. Here, wheel! Wheel!" He whistled. It sounded like an engine was whistling!

Two enormous wheels came out of nowhere and stopped in front of us. By God knows what odd art, two barrel people had affixed themselves to the middle of those wheels, where they sat gripping a peculiar nest-like seat.

Bhombol scooped me up and flung me onto the seat, similar to how people toss their portmanteaus or bags into a motorcar. Then he took the seat next to mine and barked "Museum. Quick!"

The wheel spun—fast! I thought I might be hurled off at any moment, so I held onto the seat for dear life. The giant wheels moved like the Punjab Mail. My throat constricted and it became almost impossible to breathe. How someone could travel while sitting in these chairs baffled me. Bhombol appeared completely unperturbed. He had his teeth out in that stupid grin and seemed to be enjoying the ride. Praise be to the wheel!

It came to an abrupt halt. Unable to maintain my balance, I was catapulted from my seat onto something soft and squishy. The next moment the squishy thing flung me off too. It said in a whining, annoyed tone, "What type of person are you?"

I must have fallen on someone. I hurriedly rose to my feet and began to apologize: "Excuse me, I'm—"

"Can you not see that I am not in my barrel? Have you lost your eyesight?"

I recovered my concentration and breath. Looking around, I spied a barrel rolling aimlessly on the ground. Addressing myself to it apologetically, I said, "Please, I'm not used to these wheels, I have never seen one before in my life, so—"

"What an idiot! He is conversing with the barrel," the voice said. "If you must converse with someone, sir, why not with me?"

I turned to my right to see a gloopy jelly-like substance lying on the road. From the middle of it an infuriated face glared at me. The face repeatedly puffed up like a football, only to deflate the next second.

Bhombol was laughing away—so hard that his eyes were watering. When he eventually regained his composure after great effort, he said, "Amal, you jumped this fellow in the middle of the street, so he has lost all his energy. Hey, Nasu, this human did not do it on purpose, so just calm down. And by the way, it is quite inappropriate to come out of your shell in the middle of the street—ha ha!"

Nasu grimaced: "Such words from you! We will see when it happens to you! Do you think I am a river or pond that anyone can just hop onto me? Go on, go, I'll need a few minutes to collect myself." Saying this he slid into his barrel, ejected three legs, and sprinted away.

Bhombol said: "Here we are at the museum. Go, take a thorough look inside. Manke," he said to a museum guard, "take this gentleman and show him around."

Since Bhombol was addressing me informally, I did the same: "Bhombol, where are you off to?"

"To the restaurant! I will collapse if I do not eat something soon. Explore it all and then come see me." He didn't even stop for a response, so he must have smelled food somewhere.

My stomach was rumbling from hunger too. I thought of going to the restaurant with him, but I doubted that my money would work in these parts. How would I pay for food? Having reached this conclusion, I followed the guide called Manke straight into the museum.

There was no end to the things I discovered and marvels I saw that day! I saw many technical drawings from the hands of the creator of these weird beings. These drawings demonstrated how our human body was transformed into theirs, how their bones were extracted from their bodies, and how their brain capacities were enhanced with chemicals, among other things. There is no use in discussing any of it, as none of it makes sense without his drawings.

There were also a lot of surreal stone statues. These statues demonstrated the transformation process and how their bodies first looked when the process began. In another exhibit, I saw a mysterious device labeled "Human Egg Incubator." Next to it was an enormous egg, at least as large as an ostrich egg, with the words "human egg" written on it. I was puzzled. I had heard of people talking about a horse's egg in jest, but never had I heard of a human egg. How fantastic! I spent a considerable amount of time attempting to comprehend how the machine worked, what the egg was, and the point of it all, but nothing made sense. I concluded after some time that this was all some kind of elaborate joke. There should be no space for such an object in a scientific museum.

In a different room I came across a statue of Chandrasen. Chandrasen—the creator deity of these beings. That colossal statue did not inspire the slightest awe or reverence. It was a figure stooping from age, the figure of a skinny, wiry old man. In that frail body shone two eyes that seemed power-hungry and completely crazed. It was a nightmare. In fact, it seemed as though his crazed eyes were glaring directly at me with malice, allowing no intruders into his domain.

The light was fading in the room. I turned around and found Manke standing there in silence. As soon as I attracted his attention, he cautioned, "Do not linger in this room for too long."

"Why?"

Manke seemed a bit nervous: "No one comes here after dark."

"But why?"

He pointed at the statue and said: "Because of him."

I re-examined the statue. A thin beam of light from a window was shining on the lips of Chandrasen's statue. It seemed to me a bloodthirsty grin was forming on those lips.

I turned and asked Manke: "But why be scared of him? He is only stone."

He replied: "The statue comes to life at night. We can all hear someone pacing back and forth in the room with the heavy thud of stone. Let us go, now."

I did not believe him, of course, but I no longer wanted to remain in this room, or even this museum. I departed and went in search of Bhombol.

Arriving at the restaurant, I found that Bhombol had caused quite a stir. Twenty or thirty empty plates were piled in front of him, and he was drinking directly from a pitcher. Seeing me come in, he banged on his table merrily: "Here you are, Amala! Come have some bhang with me!"[14]

I forced myself to swallow my irritation. I said, "I do not touch the stuff. But I must be back before sunset. Take me back."

He jumped up at once and said: "Ah, so glad you reminded me! Let me drop you off. Otherwise that grumpy old man will get annoyed and will not let me marry his daughter!"

"What do you mean by that? Are you going to marry her?"

"Oh you didn't know? I am engaged to be married to Kamala!"

Kamala! This hideous ogre was to wed that stunning girl? What a bizarre idea!

Bhombol said: "Listen, do not tell the old man that I drink bhang. I will make your life a living hell if you dare speak up about this."

We made our way out of the restaurant. Bhombol was too inebriated to use only three legs, so he pulled out an extra three and started to walk with me. Then he shot out four hands, too, and began to clap and sing:

"Hey, he may be Amala
But he ain't a koala
Let's beat him with a paddle
(Paddle, paddle)
His name is Amala!

His legs are but two,
His brain's empty too,
He is too full of poo,
Let's turn him upside down!
Let's make Amala frown!

Gets thrown from a wheel
He talks in a squeal
His face, now—what's the deal?
Green banana is his meal!

Hey, he may be Amala
But he ain't a koala
Let's beat him with a paddle
(Paddle paddle)
His name is Amala!"

I was quite irritated and I wanted to slap him, but he was so intoxicated that it would have made no difference at all. So, I kept my cool and let him finish his offensive song uninterrupted.

10 I Will Be a New Human

A bird song woke me up the next morning. An exquisite colorful bird sat on the windowsill fluttering its tail and singing melodiously. The sight of a familiar bird from the outside world made my heart swell with joy. Thank the heavens that Chandrasen had not decided to augment birds, too, with his evil arts.

The lovely Kamala came into my room. She seemed a bit glum.

I enquired: "What happened, Kamala? Are you unwell?"

She said: "No, it's just that my father is angry with me."

"Why?"

"Because I have put on this form. He says that I am sinning by not living in my barrel. Is that true?"

"If you do not want to, why should you have to?"

"I am of the same opinion. But my father just does not understand this. He is quite conservative and obstinate. He also told me that you cannot change shape like we do—not even a little? That your body is full of bones, and that you cannot roll. Is that all true?"

"It is."

"And you have no barrel at all?"

"Not at all! Only tortoises, crabs, oysters and the like live in shells where I come from."

"I have read about your species in history books, but never seen one in the flesh. OK, tell me, is everyone like this where you come from?"

"Yes."

"I like how you look. Tell me, are the women beautiful there?"

"Yes, but they are not as beautiful as you."

She liked that and started laughing.

I went over to the window and pointed at a particular building about which I'd been wondering. I asked her: "What is that place over there, Kamala?"

She took a look and said: "That is the hatchery."

"What is that?"

"You are quite silly—that is where babies are born. Now, since I am struggling with my posture, I need to return to my barrel. I do not want to show you my true form, because if I do so you will laugh at me." She exited with her jet-black hair swirling behind her.

I closed my eyes and thought about the hatchery. What could it be? Was this another of Kamala's pranks?

I was lost in such odd thoughts when I heard two voices: the Science Master and someone else. I was going to get up, but then I felt it might be better to eavesdrop. It took me little time to understand that the topic of conversation was myself. They must have thought I was asleep.

The anonymous voice said: "Science Master, this sample of yours is going to be difficult."

He replied: "True. But if we can achieve something great with this one, then we will be even more famous. I am quite certain that I'd be able to achieve my goals with just one surgery."

"And then what?"

"Then all we need is more human test subjects. We can prolong our life-force infinitely with this process. We have run out of options. Our life-force has grown terribly feeble after all these centuries of isolation."

"Will we inform him about all this before the surgery?"

"Amarchandra, you are naïve. Amal would not be pleased at all if he learns of our plans."

"What do you plan to do, then?"

"I shall begin by slicing through his whole body along its length. Then I will electrify his body and carefully extract all his bones one by one."

I had been silently listening to everything up until this point, but I almost yelled in horror when I heard this. You moon-faced old monster, so this was your diabolical plan all along!

Amarchandra said: "Science Master, do you recall you tried the process last year with that Turkish fellow? The king issued an edict prohibiting anyone from attempting these experiments ever again."

"I have no memory lapses. But I will be stealthy about the experiment this time. If I am successful, the king will not be upset with me at all. My failure was the source of all the uproar."

"Yes, but keep in mind that many other scholars in this land are your enemies too. And Bhombol, who has a great deal of influence at the court, is not your friend either."

The Science Master replied: "I am aware of everything already. You will be here on the day of the procedure, right?"

"Absolutely! I will enlist Pramod's help too."

"Yes, that would be useful. He is quite handy with scalpels."

Amarchandra said: "I pray to God for your success this time. May the spirit of Chandrasen guide us."

With this, the two devils left the room.

*

So that was the plan. Slice my body open, pump me with electricity, and extract my bones. An experiment? What a lovely idea. My whole body felt numb. Scared? This was beyond scary. It was as if my heart had completely squeezed in and become dry as tanned leather.

I heard footsteps in the room again. Who would it be now? I would die of fright in this place, it seemed. Every second seemed to unfold a new danger. What an abominable country!

I lay there completely still, waiting.

The next minute I heard the booming voice of Bhomboldas: "Hey Amal, do people sleep till noon back in your country too?"

I sat upright. I still had not forgotten his disrespectful song from yesterday. My name is Amala? He will paddle me? Really now!

He was staring at me with his dumb fish-like eyes. He must have sensed my displeasure. He came closer and said, "Come on, Amal! I was a bit intoxicated yesterday and sang a ridiculous song. Such things can occur between buddies. Do not be grumpy about such things."

I frowned even more. Honestly, that this odd monster even considered me a friend only intensified my disgust. I am going to befriend such monsters—hah, piss off!

Bhombol said again, "Amal, brother, come on, are you really unwilling to forgive me? Look, here are eight hands, I'm going to fold them all in penitence. I will not sing songs about you again. If you like, I can also produce four or five noses . . ."

It became apparent why he was doing all of this! He was afraid I would inform the Science Master about his drug habits, and his engagement to Kamala would be broken off. He probably couldn't stand me one bit. Anyway, since I had him in my grasp, there was no point in letting him escape. In this awful kingdom, I would have to use all the help I could get, or, in other words, use a thorn to remove a thorn.

So I said to him: "OK, so you promise not to sing such songs again?"

"Never, never! Triple promise!"

"Ok, I forgive you this time."

"So you will not tell anyone about last evening?"

"No. But I have a question: do you have influence at the court here?"

"Yes, a lot! The king loves me!"

"Do you know someone called Amarchandra?"

"Yes, quite well. But why do you ask?"

"And you do not much like this Amarchandra and the Science Master, am I right?"

His face turned ashen. "How did you hear of this?"

I replied: "The source does not matter. But tell me, is it OK to conduct experiments on live human bodies?"

Bhombol replied: "Well, it all depends on who is being cut and who is doing the cutting. Say for instance someone wanted to cut me, I'd yell and scream so much even the heavens would hear me. But if it were your body, I might not mind at all."

I rolled my eyes: "Is that so?"

He stammered: "No, no brother. Just kidding."

"This is worse than your song from yesterday."

"Whatever you say, brother. You have no sense of humor. Once upon a time I cut off someone's four arms. They didn't say a thing."

"Why would they? They can just grow eight more in their place."

"That is true. But see, Amal, this reminds me. Sometime ago there was a Turk who came to our kingdom by mistake. The Science Master dissected him for experimentation."

I replied, feigning innocence: "Why?"

"I am not entirely sure why. But rumors circulated that he was trying to create a being that was even superior to us."

I shuddered. "Then?"

"Thereafter nothing! There was no new human. It was only the poor Turk that lost his life in the whole process. Since then, there is a law that if such experiments are to be conducted on anyone, the subject must give their consent."

I breathed a sigh of relief. A huge weight was lifted off my shoulders. Even if the Science Master came to speak to me in the sweetest of his voices and said: "Amal, you are such a good boy. I want to cut your body into long strips and conduct some experiments. I hope you are OK with it," I would surely not agree and say: "Yes of course, your wish is my command. Why wait, just bring your surgical instruments, let's do the honors!"

Bhombol said: "Come to think of it, for the last few days I have seen this Amar fellow and the Science Master whispering about something. They must be up to something again."

I hid my true opinions and said: "No, no, it can't be. The Science Master seems such a kind, sagacious, being!"

"Kind? Sagacious? You are bad with people it seems. He is a Juju! The Science Master is a wicked old Juju! Anyway, let it be. Do you want to go out?"

"Again?"

"No worries, we will not go to that restaurant. Nor will I sing any songs."

"Then where will we go?"

"To the ministerial court! There is a debate today."

"OK, sure. I will ask the Science Master first. We need his consent, after all."

11 The Human Egg, Once Again

While we drink tea in the late afternoon, these creatures drink a sherbet made of spicy chili peppers. The Science

Master had remarked: "We drink spicy sherbet to remind ourselves that the world is not a cheerful place."

I had discovered how miserable the world was just by being imprisoned in the Juju country. I had no need to sample their concoction to make matters worse.

That evening I bumped into Kamala as she was panting from her chili sherbet. She asked: "So, how do I look today, in my blue saree?"

"Splendid!"

She asked, out of the blue: "Amal-babu, how do the children look back in your home country?"

I tried to describe them as accurately as possible.

She asked: "Do you have any children?"

"No."

She seemed a bit crestfallen: "I don't have any either. You cannot purchase a child here before turning 25."

I was rendered speechless with wonder. After a little pause, I replied: "You buy and sell children here?"

"Yes, we do. The younger the child, the more expensive it is. My father purchased me when I was two years old."

The Science Master joined us, so we ceased our conversation. But I resolved to inquire about it with Bhombol the next time we met. This seemed quite mysterious.

Bhombol dropped in at the usual hour. On the way to the court, I questioned him: "So, Kamala said she was purchased by her father when she was two. What does that mean?"

"It means exactly what it means! Wait—I see why you might be puzzled. Here's how it works. When Chandrasen made us, he figured out that if we continued to be born in the conventional manner as inferior, weak humans, we would not all evolve equally to supremacy at the same rate. Think about it: Your parents and children do not have the same mental or physical abilities. Therefore, he determined that we must become oviparous."

I could not believe my ears: "Eggs? You lay eggs?"

"Yep, we lay eggs. And every single one of them is scientifically analyzed. The inferior or damaged eggs are discarded, while the healthy ones are cared for in the hatchery. Which is also where the eggs hatch."

"But why do those who lay eggs not care for them?"

"That would be illegal. The penalties are quite severe for any male or female discovered hiding their eggs."

"Male or female?"

"Yes, both men and women lay eggs."

"Even males lay eggs here?"

"Of course!"

"And then what?"

"The hatchery takes care of our young after they have hatched. Once we reach the age when we may purchase a child, we simply do so and bring it home."

I was too overwhelmed with wonder at all this new information to bring myself to ask any more questions before we reached the ministerial court.

The ministerial courthouse was a gigantic, spherical structure. I was thoroughly patted down at the entrance by a few sepoys. They took everything they deemed inappropriate before allowing me to pass. I was told I could retrieve my things when I left.

I questioned Bhombol: "Why such strict precautions?"

He grinned his usual grin, all teeth bared: "The general populace dislikes the ministerial court."

The main hall was deserted, with the exception of one barrel-person who was snoring contentedly upon the dais. In front of him I spotted a brass pipe.

Bhombol informed me: "That pipe is how the peace is kept at these meetings. You might even see it in use today."

The hall does not need much description. Its main distinguishing feature was that it was shaped like a spiral tower rising from the center of the room. There was not a single chair in sight. The barrel-people, who come, sit themselves all around the tower's spirals, and settle in, don't need chairs. Simple as that.

The sleeping barrel suddenly came to life and rang a gong. As soon as he did so, doors opened on all sides of the hall, and numerous barrel-folk rushed into the chamber. They quickly settled themselves in their allotted spaces, and a hushed silence fell.

The barrel in the center spoke out: "Let the work of the court begin!"

Instantly about a dozen barrels jumped up and began yelling, while flailing their arms and making bizarre facial gestures. As soon as they fell silent, another group stood up and started doing the same. Looking at Bhombol nodding, I assumed he was able to follow whatever it was that was going on in the room. But I could make neither head nor tail of anything they said.

I asked: "When will the debates begin?"

"I have never met another as stupid as you," he said. "This is the debate."

"But how? They are all chattering together . . ."

"How else are they supposed to talk? If each of us took a turn, how would we ever find enough time to say everything we want to say?"

"But can you even understand each other in this cacophony of voices?"

"There is absolutely no need to understand."

"So how can anyone decide how to vote on the issues?"

He looked at me pityingly and said: "You are so naïve. Everyone votes strictly along party lines, so there is no need to understand any other viewpoints."

"So why waste your time engaging in a sham of a discussion?"

"Looks like I'm in painfully stupid company. What does it mean to be civilized, if not speaking publicly about important issues?"

"So you have no obligation to listen to the other party, only speak?"

"Indeed. No one here wants to listen to the other party. They want to express their own ideas. This is how civilization works."

The central barrel had begun to snore again, but it snapped out of it and hit the gong. Instantaneously, all the barrels raced to one side of the room or another with great commotion.

I asked again: "What is happening now?"

He replied: "They are voting, obviously."

Out of nowhere, a brawl broke out between the two parties. The barrel in the middle must have been trying to sleep yet again, but it suddenly got up and stood all alert.

Directing its brass pipe in the direction of the disturbance, it pressed a button. The device fired a little ball, which landed in the middle of the fight and detonated. Three barrel-people fell to the ground at once, no longer even recognizable—their bodies had disintegrated completely.

"Oh my, would you look at that!" remarked Bhombol, casually. "Old man Deben has turned to dust!"

The fighting ceased immediately.

I asked, fearfully: "Bhombol, are they really dead?"

"Yeah, they're dead," he replied. "There was no other means of maintaining order. It was Deben's fault—he couldn't resist starting a fight every time we had these assemblies. Now it's all over for him. But—you look pale—what's upsetting you?"

I replied: "I salute your great system. Now please just get me out of here."

12 Looming Threats

I could not get the ugly incident at the court out of my mind. I felt completely defeated. Even once I'd returned to the house of the Science Master, I didn't feel any better. There was a violin mounted on the wall of my room, so I picked it up and started to play. I was a prisoner in this godforsaken land. There was a sword hanging above my head at every moment—because the murderous Science Master wanted to dissect me for his secret experiments. Was it surprising that I should absentmindedly play a sad melody on this mournful-sounding instrument?

When I'd finally stopped playing, I felt a warm drop of liquid splash on my neck. Startled, I turned around to find

Kamala standing just behind me. I'd been so immersed in my music that I'd completely missed her entrance. Her large eyes were filled with tears as they gazed upon me. I asked: "Kamala! Why do you weep?"

She brushed away her tears and asked, shyly: "Why were you playing such a depressing tune? It made me cry!"

I laughed and said: "Very well, let us turn this into something joyful. You can sing a happy song, and I can play for you. Will you sing?"

"Sure, why not. Here we go:

> The moon in the sky at night,
> Floats away in the river bright.
> The wind sings in my ear,
> Songs of love I hear.
>
> The red and blue flowers shine,
> Lift their heads up to mine.
> Their fragrant dreams,
> Hide in moonbeams.
>
> Birds sing their soothing song,
> To calm away all the storms.
> They say to me,
> Just smile and let be,
> There's but one life for you and me.

The song ended. I exclaimed: "Kamala, you have the sweetest voice! After hearing Bhombol's horrible singing I had lost all interest in the music of this land."

"He sang for you? This is one of his most annoying habits—he forces everyone to listen to his silly songs. He imagines himself a great Ustad, as if the whole world is just waiting to hear him sing! He does the same to me every now and then—forcing me to listen to him. What a nightmare! It's like three owls, two donkeys, and a wild bobcat all yelling at once! And then he'll ask: 'Did you enjoy it?' If you politely tell him that you did, he'll grab his tanpura and start singing with even more enthusiasm!"

I burst out laughing and replied: "Ha ha, no—he has promised me he will not sing a song for me again."

"Amal-babu, then he has finally been endowed with good sense."

I said: "Kamala, why do you call me Amal-babu? Do you not want to call me dada?"[15]

"You wouldn't mind?"

"Why would I? I think of you like a younger sister!"

"Oh, that is so delightful to hear! Sometimes I wish I were exactly like you people."

"But Kamala—you do look just like us."

"No, no. I saw a picture at the museum once that I really loved, and it pleases me to imitate it with this form. But I cannot do it for long. Since we lack bones, our bodies begin to ache quite soon if we hold a particular form for too long. Then we have to slip back into our ugly barrels again. Chandrasen was wrong to tinker with our bodies. You like me right now, in this form, and you even think of me as a sister—but if you saw me in my barrel-body form you would be disgusted, right?"

"It isn't disgust, Kamala. I'm just not used to seeing bodies like yours. It's startling, but not repulsive."

"You're just being polite. I've seen how you look at us. It is not just surprise I discern on your face, but fear and contempt."

"What I'm afraid of, Kamala, is your father. Like Chandrasen, he wants to experiment on my body and turn me into an inhuman."

"I had no idea!" she gasped. "But I have noticed, these last few days, that he's been acting quite suspiciously."

"Why do you say that?"

"I've heard that we had a Turkish visitor a while ago, and he killed that poor man by trying to do something along those lines. His face now has the same expression it did then."

"Then listen, Kamala. You are like a sister to me, so I will not hide anything from you." I told her about the recent exchange I'd overheard between the Science Master and Amarchandra.

She was struck dumb with horror. Then she said, excitedly: "Can he really be so cruel? But don't worry—I'll help you. Conducting experiments on living subjects is forbidden by law here. Once I tell the right people about this, they will not let my father do such wicked things."

A deep, angry voice interrupted us: "Is that so?"

We whirled around. The Science Master stood in the doorway. His eyes flashed with fiery anger, and his eyeballs were popping several arms' lengths out of their sockets and back in again. So this is how the people of this land express their rage!

13 Kamala's Barrel

That ill-fated moment that had made me lose my will to live was right here, personified in this figure standing in front of me. The Science Master had overheard Kamala.

He had heard, too, that I knew about his vile plans. There was no escape.

The Science Master's face reminded me of Bhombol's words: "Juju. The Science Master is a wicked old Juju!" He looked like the devil incarnate, a bloodsucking monster.

He mocked Kamala: "Daughter mine has become a guardian angel! She will not let her father commit sins! She will save the life of this foreign animal by denouncing and disgracing her father! Hah, what a goody two-shoes!"

Kamala just stood there with her eyes downcast. Her face was pallid with fear.

The Science Master said: "Your mind has become warped thanks to your ridiculous practice of copying these animals. I'd feared as much, but I had no idea it had gone this far. You do know how children who disobey or disrespect their parents are punished, here, don't you?"

She said: "But you cannot murder Amal-dada!"

He grimaced with rage: "Amal-dada! You have the audacity to call this primitive imbecile your brother to my face! That does it—I am going to end your nonsense right now."

The Science Master moved swiftly to stand before her. He waved his hands in a strange way. Kamala started to writhe in agony, as if her whole body was being tortured. Though she did her best to hide it, a look of extreme fear appeared on her face.

Kamala collapsed to the ground, nothing but a shapeless blob of muscle and fat. She reminded me of the naked barrel-person I'd fallen on in front of the science museum.

The Science Master hissed at the shapeless mass and said sternly: “Why do you not try calling for your Amal-dada? He will not even glance at you now.”

My ears were red with rage. I looked at the shapeless mass, from which two eyes looked back at me sadly. Her form had changed indeed, but her eyes were the same. I replied affectionately: “He’s wrong, Kamala. Just because you have lost your form does not mean I no longer think of you as a sister!”

The Science Master laughed cruelly: “Oh really, the silly sister has a silly brother! Wonderful!” He called to a servant outside the room: “Hey you, bring Kamala’s barrel at once!”

A bigger barrel came at once holding a small barrel.

The Science Master said: “Kamala! Get into your barrel this instant!”

She pleaded mournfully: “Please, please, father! Do not make me get into the barrel in front of Amal-dada! I will die of shame!”

The Science Master barked: “Get in! Now! If you die of shame that is fine by me! Get in!”

Three hands and three legs protruded from the shapeless mass, which then slid into the barrel. The barrel-face looked a bit like the Kamala I knew, but unlike her at the same time.

The Science Master said: “I command you! For a whole month you are forbidden to leave your barrel. Now go to your room.”

Her arms and legs reabsorbed, Kamala rolled slowly out of the room.

The one friend I had in this cruel enemy kingdom, the one who'd been there through all my hardships and imprisonment, the only one who could have really helped me, was now a helpless prisoner herself. No one else would even care about me anymore. My life was forfeit.

The Science Master looked at me and said: "Now it is your turn."

I replied with quiet determination: "Then get started."

"I saved your life. I gave you shelter. And this is how you repay me?"

I replied: "I do not believe I have done anything wrong."

He shouted at me: "Oh you don't, eh? Perhaps where you come from it isn't a serious offense to cause a daughter to disobey her father, but here it is. What's more, children here who disrespect or disobey their parents are subject to capital punishment!"

"I didn't know!" I protested. "Don't tell me about it. I assure you, I have never asked Kamala to disobey you."

"You really expect me to believe that? Do you think I am as stupid as you inferior creatures? Has my brain evaporated like camphor? Do you think Kamala would dare to defy her father if you hadn't poisoned her against me? Against the one who saved your life?"

This was intolerable. I said: "Stop crediting yourself for saving my life. Do you think I'm in the dark about your true motivations for rescuing me? You plan to murder me at your leisure."

He flew into a rage: "I have no more time to waste on you. I will lock you up. There will be no more mercy for you."

14 The Real Face of Bhomboldas

I lay in my room alone, drowning in the well of my misfortune. I could dream no dream of escape. My one and only chance had been with Kamala, but she too was now a prisoner. She would no longer be able to expose the Science Master's nefarious plan. Everything in this weird, wretched country has been twisted—kindness, affection, and love all have a different face.

On the topic of different faces, I thought about legends I'd heard, from various parts of the world, about ghosts and spirits who assume different shapes to scare people. They come out at night and play their tricks, and then disappear again at daylight—no one knows where they originate, and no one knows where they vanish to. I believe these barrel-people are the origin of such stories, and perhaps this land is the hell that people imagine awaits us after death. Bhombol, for example, assumed my face right in front of my eyes—maybe these barrel-people take on the shape of our dead relatives and ancestors, while visiting the outside world, thus creating a belief in ghosts.

They call themselves "new humans." That's utter rubbish! There can be no humanity in a barrel.

I heard a voice calling out to me softly: "Amala, oh Amala!"

Outside my window, I saw the hideous, wart-covered face of Bhombol.

I retorted: "You know that is not my name. Are you here to cheer my execution?"

He said: "Come on, brother, why do you get annoyed so easily? I told you that both men and women here lay eggs—so to us, 'Amal' and 'Amala' are interchangeable names. But come close to the window, so we won't be overheard. I'll get right to the point."

Though I knew he was a useless fellow, I went over to the window to hear him out.

"I have not given up on you," Bhombol whispered. "I have spoken to many influential people who cannot stand the Juju. But so far I have not met with much success. You are nobody here, no one even knows your name. Nobody will go up against the Science Master for a mere foreigner. He has a lot of power, so people assume that he is a patriot—and that whatever he is planning to do must be for the benefit of our country."

I said: "You did not have to come all this way just to bring me this bad news."

He replied with his usual grin: "I know I didn't have to come all this way—but I couldn't help myself. You are, after all, my friend. But I have good news too, Amala. I was able to arrange a hearing with the king himself. If you have any strong reasons as to why you should not be dissected, then he is willing to hear your plea. If you can persuade him you might survive. That's the good news: No one can dissect you without presenting you to the king first."

I replied gratefully, "Brother Bhombol, thank you for so much helping me! This is indeed great news!"

Bhombol replied: "No need to thank me yet. First, let us see whether you survive this, then we can see about the thanks. Well, all this has made me very hungry. To a restaurant I go!"

I began to believe that Bhombol was not so terrible after all. Despite his ugly features and rude manners, his barrel-body has a heart and soul. Bhombol seems to be like a mango, misshapen on the outside, but pure sweetness within!

I thought he had left, but his face popped up again. He glanced both ways and then whispered: "There is one more thing. Sorry, I forget things when I'm hungry. Take this and conceal it on your person. If you get into a pickle, just press the knob at the back." He handed me a small brass pipe, grinned again, and vanished.

I gingerly inspected the pipe. It appeared to be the same sort of deadly instrument I'd seen deployed at the ministerial court. The one Bhombol gave me was easy to conceal. OK, at least I was armed now.

Hearing someone at the door, I hastily hid the pipe in my pocket. The door opened to reveal Amarchandra, the Science Master, and four other barrel-people.

"Amal, you must come with us," the Science Master grated.

Thank goodness, they were going to present me to the king. Assuming this was the case, I left my chambers without making a fuss. The Science Master and Amarchandra led the line, two barrels guarded me from the sides and two others watched me from the rear. They had no intention of letting me escape.

15 My Great Courage

The chamber to which I was taken was the one where I'd first opened my eyes in this strange land. It had once again been transformed into a laboratory—or an operating room. At the center of the room was the long table on which I'd been stretched. It was surrounded by surgical equipment and all manner of medicinal concoctions, glass bottles and glass utensils!

Looking me over carefully, Amarchandra wasn't satisfied. "It's too soon," he said doubtfully. "This one's body isn't sufficiently prepared for the surgery—I don't think it's going to work."

The Science Master said: "It makes no difference to me. I will do this today."

Fear gripped me as I said: "Wait, why have you brought me here?"

"Today is the day I experiment on you."

"What do you mean?" I cried indignantly. "Do you not know that the king has ordered you to take me to him first?"

"Indeed?" The Science Master was startled. "And where have you heard this?"

"It doesn't matter! Take me to your leader!"

Amarchandra chortled: "I can guess who has been scheming behind our backs. We have many enemies in the court. If we take you there, we may well end up without a test subject!"

"You refuse to listen to your king?"

The Science Master shrugged: "We must protect the integrity of science. We don't have time for debate." Turning to the other barrel-folk, he said: "Hold him down and bind him to the table."

I launched myself at the Science Master, driven by pure rage, and kicked him with all my might. With a cry of pain he crumpled to the floor. In a frenzy, I reached for the largest knife on the operating table, the one that must have been intended to tear me to pieces, and began swinging it wildly about. The barrel-men's lack of bones made them an easy target—pieces of them were severed wherever the blade struck. Slicing them was like slicing tapioca. They howled and shrieked as the knife passed through their bodies, then fled. Their fallen body parts flopped on the floor like severed lizard tails.

I turned now to Amarchandra, who folded himself into his barrel and slithered away like a snake.

It was only me and the Science Master now. He shouted for his servants, who were nowhere to be seen. I roared: "So, old Juju! Who will save you now? Come let me perform some surgery on you!" I sprang at him with my knife. His eyes rolled up into the back of his head and his face turned pale as a ghost. Many legs uncurled out of his barrel, and he scuttled off like a spider. Though I chased him around the room, with two legs it's tricky to catch a creature with a bunch of them. I don't know how long we would have danced this dance had the door not slammed open. A group of new barrel-folk came crashing in, with Bhomboldas leading the way.

One of the barrel-folk spoke in a grave voice: "What is the meaning of all this?"

The Science Master replied: "Please, Your Majesty! Save me!"

The King was enormous; his barrel dwarfed even Bhomboldas's. It was an even bigger and fatter barrel than the kind we use to mix cement back home. His cheeks were swollen like gourds and his long trailing mustache nearly touched the floor. Really? This was their ruler?

Eyes the size of gooseberries protruded from the King's enormous face and bore down on me. They scrutinized me from every angle for a couple of minutes, before receding into his eye sockets. "Are you a madman?" he asked, in a regal tone. "Looking at you makes Us wonder."

I smiled a wan smile: "No, Your Majesty! Unfortunately, I have not yet been able to go mad. But I imagine I will be able to quite soon."

The King oscillated. "We are delighted to hear that," he said. "Those who have no hope of going mad are most unlucky. Regardless, We are extremely fatigued with all Our walking. We are parched. Servant, fetch Us some spring water now."

The servant presented him with water. The King swallowed the contents of the pitcher in a gulp and belched with satisfaction. He continued: "Ah, that was refreshing. Back to business. So, Bhomboldas, is this the foreigner you were pleading for? What is his name?"

Bhombol flashed his grin at me and replied: "Amala."

I piped up: "No, Your Majesty! My name is Amal, not Amala!"

The King snapped at me: "Silence, fool! We know Bhomboldas a lot better than We know you. He has the authority to choose the name you deserve. Looking at you today, We are certain that Amala is a much better name for you. Oh my, it is sweltering here. Servants, why are you not fanning Us?"

Two barrel-folk immediately began fanning the king with large palm leaves.

After cooling down, the King began to oscillate again. He asked: “So, Amala, was that a war dance you were doing for the Science Master? We enjoyed it! Come, dance for Us again!”

I clasped my hands in submission: “Not at all, Your Majesty! I was teaching him the ins and outs of surgery!”

The King roared at me: “What! Do you not know We have outlawed all surgical procedures! We only go for Ayurvedic medicinal practices here, nothing else will do! Instead of wasting your time on surgery, you should tell the Science Master to consume some potions!”

I apologized to the King and said: “I didn’t remember about the potions, Your Majesty.”

The Science Master was trying to make himself heard, but the King cut him off: “Silence, you old fool! Do you not know that you should not speak to Us unless spoken to? Oh, Our ears are itching. Servants, get me an earbud now!”

The servant barrels brought him a large earbud. The King relaxed for five minutes, twisting it around in his ear. Suddenly he pulled it out and yelled: “So what was going on?”

I replied: “Your Majesty, did you know that the Science Master was about to operate on me? He was planning to cut my body into strips and conduct his experiments.”

The King exploded in rage: “What! Without first presenting you to Us?”

“Indeed, Your Majesty! He said he was going to honor science instead of you!”

"My, such grand words!" raged the King. "Won't honor Us indeed! My head is spinning! Servants, stop my head from spinning."

The King's head was indeed whirling, and fast! I could hardly discern his facial features. Servant-barrels grabbed his head as firmly as possible from all sides, until it came to a stop.

The King wheezed for a while until he regained his breath. Then he growled: "Evil Science Master! You seek to defy Our will again and cook up new experiments! Bhomboldas, you remember when he was at it before? To think of all the trouble he caused!"

Bhomboldas replied: "Indeed, Your Majesty! I remember—the Science Master vivisected the Turk in such a way that his body looked as twisted and ugly as that of the Science Master himself!"

The Science Master protested: "No, he did not look like me! Such slander!"

The King roared again: "How dare you speak out again, Science Master! You have no right to protest here! When We decide to allow you to protest is up to Us!"

The Science Master said: "But my King, how will You know when I want to protest?"

The King scowled at the Science Master's brazenness: "Tell Us, Bhombol, just what he means? If We cannot tell him when to protest, what right do we have to call Ourselves king?"

Bhombol nodded: "Indeed, Your Majesty!"

The Science Master pleaded: "Your Majesty, I plead for justice to be done!"

"You plead for justice?" scoffed the King. "Bhombol, look, the Science Master pleads for justice! Very well. We shall hand out justice to you. Bhombol, assemble the ministerial court at once. We will pass our judgment here today. Deliver Our royal scepter!"

16 The King's Judgment

The King lifted his scepter and proclaimed: "Science Master! Tell Us why you want to dissect this inferior human? Give Us all the details—and with all the respect this occasion demands!"

The Science Master replied: "Your Majesty, it is to create a human even more advanced than us."

The King furrowed his brows: "Even more advanced than us? Are you implying that we have regressed? That we are primitive?"

"Yes, your Majesty, that is what I believe. Just imagine, my King, this Amal, this savage, will be the first to be improved. What an incredible honor! Rather than murdering him, I would have dissected him slowly—while keeping him alive. I will require no more than twenty days! My motives are pure, my King!"

The King nodded and said: "Indeed, We sense how pure your motives truly are. Amala, why do you come between the man and his pure motives?"

I replied: "No, Your Majesty! I was not trying to stop him; I was merely trying to save my own life! Would you command me to go under his knife, be sliced into bits for twenty days, be tortured alive, and not protest at all?"

"Of course not!" agreed the King. "We would never give such a cruel command."

I continued: "Furthermore, Your Majesty, this Science Master would have operated on me without Your knowledge, and against Your explicit orders! If he had done so after You gave Your order, I would have not protested in the slightest. Was his not a serious offense?"

"A heinous offense indeed! A heinous, horrible offense! Servant, bring Us the fifth volume of our laws. Let Us determine the severity of the offense."

The King was presented with the code of laws, and he pored over its pages. "Here it is! This is a violation of Section 727—the penalty is death! Science Master, you will be executed!"

The Science Master began to tremble. He fell on his knees and pleaded: "Your Majesty, please, have pity on me! If I am put to death, I will not be alive. You have not heard the whole story. This primitive man has done me great harm . . . he has turned my daughter against me!"

The King gasped: "What! There is nothing worse than a disobedient daughter! This surpasses Section 727! Amala, do you have anything to say for yourself?"

I began to fear for my life once again: "Yes, Your Majesty! However, I must start at the beginning! Yesterday I was playing the violin . . ."

"Nice, nice! So you can play the violin?"

"Yes, Your Majesty."

"And you can sing as well?"

"Yes, Your Majesty."

"Nice, nice! Then perform a song for Us."

I pleaded: "But Your Majesty, I am an Ustad![16] I require a tabla[17] and other accompaniments for my performance."

The King beckoned: "Servants! Bring a tabla."

Bhomboldas hurriedly whispered something in the King's ear.

The King turned to me again: "Amala, this is an operation theater! There are no tablas here. Do you have a solution for Us?"

I said: "I do, Your Majesty! The Science Master has round rubbery cheeks! Please command him to come here, and I will smack him left and right. That will be enough music for me."

The Science Master said: "I object! I vehemently object to this!"

The King scowled at him: "Seems you cannot stay silent. What Amala is requesting is perfectly lawful. You must obey him. I command you to act as a tabla for him."

The Science Master approached me. I was about to give him a good slap, but he kept turning his face every time I raised my hand. I told the King: "Your Majesty, the Science Master refuses to be played. He keeps turning his head!"

The King said: "Is that so? Very well! Guards, seize his head and hold him still."

The guards held the Science Master's head in a strong grip. I slapped his cheeks to establish a rhythm and began singing:

In the Juju Kingdom
  A Juju I have seen
He has little wisdom
  But he is just so mean

He is a bit ghostly, and he is a bit ghastly
He has silly manners, but all so dastardly

He lives in a round barrel,
His eyes are glowing feral
But his brain has gone sterile,
If you believe his lies,
You do it at your peril.

His love is a death sentence,
His words will test your patience
He will murder without remorse
He suffers from complacence
He may shout, he may spin
Like he's a crazy djinn
He may huff, he may puff,
Let's throw him in a loony bin

If you see him coming
Run and climb a tree
Spit on him from the treetop
Or throw your machete
Mash the Juju into pulp
Or you won't be free!

The King applauded: "Bravo, bravo! What a song! What a voice! Is it not so, Bhombol?"

He said: "Yes indeed, Your Majesty!"

The Science Master stroked his flaming cheeks and said: "My King, I protest this song . . ."

The King shook his head: "No, you cannot object to this. We will let you know when and where you may protest!"

The Science Master said: "But my King, that song was slanderous! It was all about me!"

The King said: "Do you believe you are Juju?"

"No, I don't!"

The King replied: "Then you have no reason to complain. This song is about a Juju. Is it not so, Amala!"

I replied: "Yes indeed, Your Majesty!"

Bhombol said: "Your Majesty, it is getting late, and I am getting hungry."

The King said, "Bhombol is hungry again, so we cannot postpone our judgment any longer. Science Master and Amal, here is Our judgment. Both of you have committed grave crimes. Both of you will be put to death! Ministers, choose the order of execution. But do not overthink this. Bhombol is hungry."

The Ministers said: "Amala's offense is the greater one. Let him be executed first!"

The King exclaimed: "This is why one needs ministers! Look, how easy it was to decide all this. Amala, you heard the verdict, right? Science Master, put him on the table and start your experiments at once."

These insanities were giving me a headache. The King was mad, the ministers were mad! Insanity reigned supreme in this realm. I looked at Bhombol. He grinned and gestured at my pockets.

Remembering his gift to me, I ran my hand over my trouser pockets. It was still there.

The King said: "Amala, do you have anything more to say?"

I said: "Yes, Your Majesty. I have two things left to say!"

"Go on! Bhombol is getting hungry."

"Your Majesty! The first thing is: You may no longer call me 'Amala.' The second thing is: My death sentence must be commuted!"

The King sighed: "And if We do not agree?"

I took out the pipe and aimed it at him: "Then this kingdom will be without a king."

The King shouted: "Guards! Guards!"

I said: "I will finish this if they come any closer. The throne will be empty."

The King said: "Retreat, guards! Go away, don't come any closer!"

Bhombol said: "Your Majesty, I am hungry."

The King said: "Very well! We will not call you 'Amala.' And We will not have you put to death."

I brought down the gun and said: "Glory to the King!"

He continued: "But instead of death, We banish you from our land. Leave now and never come back. You are not fit for this place. Bhombol is hungry, so We declare this session over."

17 Exile

Many barrel-folk surrounded me and snatched away my weapon. Then they hauled me to the main street. Everywhere I looked, thousands of barrels were streaming towards us. Men-barrels, women-barrels, baby-barrels, teen-barrels! I never imagined there were so many.

The barrel-folk all seemed to be furious with me! Perhaps they were infuriated that I had dared to aim a gun at their king? Rumors fly fast in this land! I was scared witless—I thought they were going to tear me to pieces. But they didn't harm me, they just came to glare at me!

The King's wheel-car went whooshing past me. The King did not even spare me a glance, but Bhombol, who sat next to him, pulled a face at me as they went past.

I shouted: "Your Majesty! Your Majesty! Please wait!"

The wheel-car came to a halt. The King spoke: "What is it now?"

I said: "I have a small complaint!"

"Go on!"

I said: "Bhombol made a face at me."

The King looked at me suspiciously: "Do you still have your gun?"

"No, Your Majesty! The guards took it away."

The King sighed with relief. "Then Bhombol may do as he pleases. He makes faces at me, too, when he is hungry. Is that not so, Bhombol?"

Bhombol pulled another face: "Yes, Your Majesty! But oh, we made a grave mistake!"

Aghast, the King asked: "Quick, what mistake? What have we done wrong?"

Bhombol replied: "We did not carry out the Science Master's sentence!"

The King smiled and said: "Not to worry. He is not going anywhere. First let Us eat and you fill yourself up. Then We can see to him. Chauffeur, let's go!"

The King's wheel sped away and disappeared into the distance.

I was blindfolded by the guards. Perhaps it was to prevent me from ever finding my way back. We traveled like this for nearly two days. When they removed the blindfold at last, I found myself back on the side of the mountain.

The guards snarled at me, "Away with you!"

Behind the guards I spied a sad face. It was Kamala—leaning against the entrance to the cave.

The guards shoved me: "Go away! Now! Run!"

I began walking away—so why wasn't I elated? Because I was leaving my sister behind. My heart wept.

THE END

VOYAGE TO VENUS (1895)

Jagadananda Ray

Because I'd had an interest in science and technology since childhood, I had gradually and with considerable effort amassed a collection of old science books and decrepit scientific instruments. My principal scientific research apparatuses were a modest, worn-out telescope, a portable aneroid barometer, and two measuring devices. I also had a bell, some test tubes, an incandescent electric bulb, a Bunsen cell, and some silk-coated wires. Together with a friend of mine who was also a science enthusiast, I spent most of my leisure time attempting to repair the telescope, the lamp, and the other antique instruments. I had planned to spend the upcoming university break doing research; however, my friend's loss of interest in our shared endeavors made this happy plan seem increasingly unlikely.

When we had first begun doing research together, my friend had come up with a novel invention for cranking a boat's engine, and had even considered patenting it. In his zeal, at significant personal expense, he had actually purchased a boat and the machine parts that he needed to construct his new engine-starter. Due to bad luck, though, the boat's engine turned out to be defective. Not only would it not start with his invention, it also failed to function with its ordinary rope-start mechanism.

Although the fault lay solely with the man who'd built the engine, my friend's interest in scientific experimentation began to wane from that moment. After another unfortunate incident in a chemical laboratory, my friend had all but lost his interest in science. Since then, I had been unable to involve him in my amateur experiments—although he did continue to discourse on scientific topics now and then. With his wide, serious countenance, enormous walrus mustache, and intimidating spectacles, few would dispute him when he spoke, nor would they dispute that here was a man guaranteed future success.

Even though I was well aware that he would not be interested in my amateurish pursuits, I still felt compelled to call on my friend one morning during my break. What he said left me even more skeptical of my chances of ever luring him back to the realm of science. It was a Sunday, so the office where he worked was closed; I tracked him down to his modest but stylishly decorated apartment. He had been working on something in the far corner of the room, and as he pulled out a chair for me, his bearing gave me the impression that he was happy. When I inquired about what he'd been working on, he responded matter-of-factly: "I was trying to write a short story for one of these monthly periodicals. After reading a few tales I decided to try and write one myself. It is almost completed, but somehow I cannot think of a proper ending."

I was quite surprised to observe the change in my friend and his pursuit of completely unscientific activities. It was quite unpopular for a scientist to turn to literature:

as a matter of fact it was my status-conscious friend who had informed me of this, so there was all the more reason for my surprise. I now saw that finely bound volumes of Shakespeare, Shelley, Tennyson, Michael Madhusudan Dutt, Rabindranath Tagore, and Bankim Chandra Chattopadhyay had replaced the hefty scientific texts that had previously crowded his desktop. With his usual enthusiasm, my friend read his story to me. I do not recall the tale very well, not because I have a poor memory but because I was so distracted by this new incarnation of my friend. I do remember, quite vividly, that upon being asked for suggestions regarding the story, I mumbled something about its 'tragic ending' that was totally off the mark—so my friend had brushed off my suggestion with a sarcastic quip about my total lack of literary sensibility. I realized that it would be difficult to get my friend interested in my scientific experiments unless I managed to get him to talk about something scientific, so I shifted the conversation to other topics—the possibility of getting a new job, the reasons behind the office superintendent's recent transfer, and so on, until I finally brought up Edison's new phonograph.

I figured that my friend would resist this turn to science- and technology-talk if literature was indeed all he now cared about, but discovered that he was as keen to speak about scientific matters as ever, including suggesting design improvements to the phonograph and insisting that more research was needed before it would become truly useful—illustrating his points with examples and possibilities that were the offspring of his vivid imagination. Finding his interest in science and technology unabated, I continued to steer the discussion towards such subjects, including the Paris exhibition, the construction of the Eiffel Tower, and finally, my own motives for having visited him. He seemed less excited at the prospect of continuing our work. He lectured me at length on the weakness of the Bengali race, our lack of originality, and how any kind of research without access to the finest instruments was a total waste of time in this day and age. Although I was able to persuade him to visit me by arguing that staying busy with scientific pursuits was preferable to wasting time, he pointed out that his doctors had advised him to stay away from taxing mental activity because of a recent illness, so he would not be working with instruments. Realizing that conducting research would be impossible, under this restriction, we agreed instead that we would review some new scientific research.

I spent the most of the following two days studying recent scientific findings, and on the third day—when my friend was due to visit—I sat wondering whether he had gone to work instead. As a volunteer, he regarded his labor as a favor to the government, and therefore he did not think it essential to show up on all six working days. In fact, he soon appeared bearing nothing but a little book by a famous English astronomer, which contained some fresh information about planets, moons, and other celestial bodies; we decided to use it as a basis for our discussions. My friend started reading about the planet Venus. It was a particularly hot day, though, so once my friend finished reading that chapter I did not feel like hearing another. My friend also yawned many times as he relaxed in a reclining chair; he flipped through the remainder of the book, then put it down. We'd both decided not to read any more. Slouching back in his recliner, my friend instead started to speak about Venus, how some scientists had theorized about the potential for life on that planet, and so on. I closed my eyes and listened.

I'm not sure how much time passed before I realized that I had arrived on the dark side of Venus. The somber silence of this land was strongly reminiscent of the peaceful solemnity of a desert night on Earth. It reminded me of something I had read—that like the Moon, one half of Venus was draped in perpetual night. The sun would never shine on this side, a realization that made the darkness appear even more gloomy. However, this everlasting night was less dark than a night on Earth, and distant stars appear brighter in the night sky of Venus. One particularly brilliant star caught my attention; spotting another, less bright object next to it, I realized it was Earth. That Earth, my own Earth, teeming with rich life, could appear so insignificant against the boundless expanse of the sky above came as a great surprise to me.

Using Earth's orbit as a guide, I was able to determine that I was somewhere near the planet's equator—and that the bright side of Venus was roughly 1200 miles away. Initially, mesmerized by the splendor of the night sky, I had forgotten all about my surroundings, but soon the cold weather made it impossible to remain outdoors any longer. I was wearing warm clothing, but they were of little protection there, so I had to seek shelter. I chose a direction at random, and started to walk briskly. The awful sound that my footsteps produced as I walked on this planet grated on my ears, despite the fact that my quick pace was helping me warm up considerably. My steps sounded louder than the hooves of numerous horses pulling a chariot. Another thing struck me about this planet—despite the intense cold, there was a complete absence of any snow or ice.

I attempted to distract myself by considering such strange, otherworldly, unnatural phenomena, but my mind did not feel at ease. My unexpected, unplanned appearance upon a strange world contrasted strongly with my previous life and the comforts of home; I was prevented from thinking properly. I also felt the absence of my friend most keenly. If only he were there too, I would not even have to think about the strangeness of all this. Understanding particularly difficult phenomena and explaining the inexplicable was his special gift.

After trekking for a while longer, though, I lost track of my earlier thoughts. All that now consumed my mind was anxiety for my future in this alien world. I felt like a ship trapped in a sea storm, being tossed about in all directions. Worse, by the faint light of the night sky, I was now able to detect someone or something—a large shadowy figure—racing towards me. I had not seen any evidence of life on the planet so far, so this was unsettling. I remembered that I had argued with my friend a few days earlier about how life was possible only on Earth due to our planet's unique conditions, but it seemed now that my friend had been correct. While I stood there contemplating all this, the dark rushing mass assumed a distinct form and stood before me.

The creature's appearance was striking and frightening. It resembled a savage man. Its body was covered in dense black fur, its head was oversized for its body, it had long claw-like nails on both hands and feet, and it was stark naked. The strange creature in front of me began howling in such a disturbing fashion that it seemed as if the silent planet had suddenly awoken and begun to tremble in that noise.

Assuming it likely that this howling was the preamble to an assault, I prepared to defend myself, though I was certain that my frail earthling body had no chance against this creature's fangs. I awaited my fate and held my ground. But soon the creature stopped howling and instead began to gesture as if bidding me to follow it; given my helpless state, I deemed it prudent to do so. Immediately, the creature turned and started to race in a direction different from the one I had taken before. I quickly realized that the creature's normal walking pace, which had seemed like running to me, was ten times that of a human's. Thus, I followed as closely as I could. The cold climate of this part of Venus must have caused these creatures to evolve their thick coat of fur; and it was also the reason perhaps for their speed, as they needed to move quickly to stay warm.

After traveling a short while with my strange companion, I noticed a hillock in the distance. My guide kept moving towards it, and we were soon in front of it. This abrupt appearance of a hillock did not seem coincidental. Having just arrived on Venus, I did not consider myself an authority on its geological peculiarities, nor did I think that explaining the many wonders of God's creation within the limited scope of my own scientific knowledge would be anything but a display of ignorance, so I was curious to know what this hillock could be. My companion began howling again, at which a segment of the hillock lit up and more creatures like my companion emerged and also began howling. I realized they were talking about me. After conversing thus for a while, they indicated that I was to follow them inside the hill, but I felt reluctant to do so. As a child, during a particularly stormy night, I had heard folk tales from the *Arabian Nights* from my grandmother, with my head on her lap. I had created a mental picture of the land of monsters, the brave prince and the tragic princess and the evil ghouls. I remembered how scared I had been, as if the storm outside meant to pull us to that evil land, how in that storm the world seemed a very frightening place, and how I had clung to my grandmother. If that Baghdad merchant's son could face such terrors even on Earth, how could I, a mere human, be less afraid of danger on an alien planet? Although these Venusians had been courteous so far, who could be certain whether their hospitality masked a sinister purpose, or hidden motivation? I could not follow them!

Noticing my hesitation, one of them went inside and soon emerged with a lamp. He was followed by another individual, whose distinctiveness was instantly apparent to me. This was an alien world, so it seemed impossible that the creature could be of the same species as me, yet from what I could see of its clothing and movement in the light of the lamp it seemed human. I was overjoyed to find a fellow unfortunate human in this unknown kingdom, and in my excitement I hurried up to greet him. What I saw brought tears of joy to my eyes, and I hugged him. I have never in my life hugged anyone with such a force of emotion, nor do I think I have ever shouted with such joy as I did then. This individual was none other than my scientist friend! I should have recognized him from a distance, but grief and anxiety had changed his manner so much that I had not been able to. Even after receiving my embrace my friend did not show any emotion, but remained expressionless, like a statue. After I repeated his name a few times he nodded his head, and a shadow of surprised recognition appeared on his face. Perhaps he mistook me for an apparition, and all this as a dream, but I finally managed to convince him I was real. He was later embarrassed that he had been so reluctant to greet a friend—and acknowledged that it was indeed unscientific to believe a physical presence could be but a figment of the imagination.

After narrating my experiences on Venus so far, I asked my friend how he'd come to visit the planet.

He replied: "Brother, I sat in your armchair during our discussion, reflecting on the possibility of life on a new planet, how life might come to be, how it might evolve, and how it might survive. I do not know how it happened, nor do I remember the conclusion of my reflections, but by some enchantment I found myself in the foul subterranean realm where these creatures live. Have you ever heard of any scientist making a discovery in such a magical fashion? I have certainly never heard of such a thing."

I attempted to cheer my friend by arguing that it was not necessary for scientists to discover things via the scientific method, for otherwise, we would have to dismiss the work of scientists such as Le Verrier, who discovered Neptune through mathematical calculations alone. I did not notice any reaction from my friend to these words, though, because the Venusians had started howling again. I turned my head in their direction.

The Venusians began to urge us to enter their cave again; the bitter cold, and the fact that my friend appeared unharmed, made me comply with their request. My friend wanted to go back inside as well. Our guide led the way with his lamp, and we followed him. I discovered that the cave contained all that was necessary for the survival of a primitive race such as the Venusians. The cave was also quite warm. How? The lack of sunlight prevented the growth of plant life on the surface, hence there was no wood or coal for a fire. It seems the Venusians had instead harvested the hive of an insect for wax and used it as fuel. There was plenty of light in the cave.

Since his arrival on Venus, my friend had had time to observe the ways of these creatures, and he filled me in with what he knew. It seemed that they were mainly vegetarians. They grew some simple kinds of vegetable matter deep inside Venus, where the warmth of the planet's core compensated for the lack of sunlight. They had a solid grasp of agricultural science and grew various types of vegetables at varying depths, depending on the amount of heat necessary for their growth. They also hunted animals for their skins and fur, and occasionally ate their meat.

We lay down next to a fire and had begun to exchange stories when a Venusian appeared before us carrying food. It occurred to me that we had been on Venus for almost ten hours, but the novelty of our experience and the prospect of danger had kept us from feeling hungry. Seeing the food reminded me of how exhausted and ravenous I was. My friend considered it unwise to eat food cultivated by this unknown and savage people, and hence at first declined to join me. But then perhaps even his philosopher's soul succumbed to the hunger pangs of his stomach, for he agreed to eat with me. After our meal I began to smoke a cigar that I had brought with me, while my friend lay down on a fur bed and discussed his preparations for leaving the cave and traveling across Venus. He regained his enthusiasm as he spoke; it was as if he was once again the scientist interested in uncovering even the most intricate details of the cosmos and delving into its deepest mysteries. He observed the thick cloud of smoke that had gathered around me as he spoke, but I really cannot tell if that led him to some deep philosophical discovery.

After resting, we stepped outside the cave for a moment. The sense of tranquility under the vividly illuminated, galaxy-filled sky brought us immense delight. The darkness of the night embracing the endless sky was sublime;

in this faint galaxy the planet Venus seemed trapped in some profound melancholy, like an example of the Maker's childlike play. Creating all this cosmic vastness, with its galaxies and planets with their seasons, He must have through childlike simplicity forged barren Venus while contemplating something else. Yet the luckier planets together with troubled and miserable Venus took part in the same cosmic story, so that all the distant galaxies too could observe this weak and unfortunate brother with amazement and rapt wonder.

Our Earth and its moon were illuminated, and we watched the sunset on planet Earth from Venus. In the silence of the sky, the Earth glowed softly in one corner. In the endless cosmos, is the Earth indeed so small, so tiny? Then how much smaller are we mortals, and how little are our dreams, sadnesses, desires! Still, even in the face of this cosmic beauty, this Hindu-child did not feel a sense of enlightened detachment—but was reminded of his home. That tiny shimmering dot contained my sweet house with a garden, all occupying the distant corner of a land now in shadows. How pleasant my evening discussions with friends used to be on our little patch of Earth! I began to wonder when I would be able to return to that beautiful planet with its beautiful life, to my everyday routine.

My friend was lost in his own thoughts. The Moon had set by then, and from a distance we could observe the last light of Earth fading away as well. I do not know if my friend discovered some poetry of nature in all this, but judging from his rapt attention and unblinking gaze he was indeed discovering something in all this worthy of reflection. It was a novel experience seeing all the planets and celestial bodies as they disappeared in the Venusian night. Our Earth has a dense atmosphere; hence it is far more difficult to see the feeble light of smaller celestial objects from its surface. The extreme weather on Venus and lack of an atmosphere made it possible to spot the light of even faint distant objects in the clear sky. I asked my friend about the absence of snow and ice in this extreme cold, and he explained that this was due to the lack of sunlight. This explanation seemed plausible to me. The water on this side of the planet never turns into vapor due to lack of sunlight—hence phenomena such as clouds, rain, rivers, and snow are completely impossible.

We spent many days in the cave and enjoyed the generous hospitality of the uncivilized Venusians. We had no way of estimating how long we had been there, because the absence of days and nights left us with no means of calculating time. I had a pocket watch, which could only count twelve hours, after which everything became confused. We were aware that the Venus year equaled 224 Earth days and 18 Earth hours, and we remembered that we could observe the sky and notice the same stellar arrangements in 224 days, so we began to keep track of time using this method. We also observed something else. Since our arrival on Venus we seldom felt hungry. The habit of eating every day and night on Earth had been almost forgotten. In two weeks, we had only eaten thrice, but we neither felt hungry nor weak. We know that the gods became immortal and without hunger on consuming *amrita*[1], so if the lack of the necessity to consume food is characteristic of godhood, then we were certainly one step closer to that level. Our heaven described in the *Puranas* must have somehow been connected to the life on this planet, my friend opined. Deciding to investigate our wondrous lack of hunger with considerable patience, he discovered that the Venusians consumed one leafy vegetable that was particularly nutritious. One could go for food without ten days after one meal of this vegetable. We had no doubt that this was the source of our imperviousness to hunger.

We were becoming weary of being in the same location for so long, so one day my friend said: "We have seen all there is to see on the dark side of this planet. Now we should see what the other side is like." I quickly accepted his proposition. After all, I had expressed similar sentiments myself more than once, but before today my friend had been unwilling to leave the comfort of the cave.

We started to prepare for our trip. We packed suitable furs for the cold, and enough food for two months, as well as some other essentials. When the Venusians learnt of our imminent departure, they appeared quite distressed and saddened. We had not anticipated any such deep emotion from these uncivilized creatures; in fact, our first acquaintance, Ghatotkach,[2] pleaded to accompany us on our journey. Having a local companion meant a great deal on an uncharted alien planet, both for finding our way and also for other tasks, so we readily agreed. We wrapped ourselves in our fur clothing, gave Ghatotkach all our food to carry with him, and left the cave.

We determined our path based on the position of the stars, and continued eastwards by following the equatorial line. According to our calculations, we needed to travel about 1200 miles to reach the other side of the planet. The sky of Venus was always crystal-clear, so we had no difficulty at all finding our bearings. Another mystery was solved during our journey, which was the reason for the loud noise we made as we walked. After much careful analysis, we concluded that the lack of heat and strong winds was the cause of this phenomenon. Our movement agitated the motionless wind to such a degree that it produced a great sound wave.

When it was too cold or we were too fatigued to continue, we would stop in a cave, but generally we traveled at a rapid pace. Although much of it was flat, there were many tiny caves scattered throughout the landscape. At times the endless flat horizon made one feel a hopelessness that made it difficult to continue. I must add, on the other hand, that my friend's philosophical temperament was much improved. The slightest mention of science, even in this arduous journey, infused him with fresh enthusiasm for the sense of wonder and the pleasures of discovery. Even in the face of such troubles, he would try to explain some phenomena, argue for and against his own speculation, and enjoy the company of his own ideas.

Within a week we had covered more than two hundred miles on foot. At this time, we observed a massive structure in the distance. To satisfy our curiosity, we approached it. From a distance it seemed merely higher ground, but on closer approach we found it to be the ruins of a mansion. We were surprised to find such a structure in this lifeless desert, for the sophistication of the construction and the elegance of its design was evident even in this ruined state. By the artistry, we could tell that this was not constructed by our familiar Venusians. My friend speculated that Venus must have had an advanced civilization at one point in time, and perhaps back then the planet too, like Earth, may have had its regular days and nights—but some accident that had resulted in this part being covered in grim darkness must have also made this hemisphere uninhabitable, and caused the extinction of these civilized beings. Now this decaying ruin stood in this eternal darkness as testimony to their lost glory.

We kept on till we had reached a location from which we could just barely spot sunlight in the distance. In the clear Venusian sky this was a magical sight. We had not seen such serene beauty ever since our arrival on the planet. It was like the faint glow of dawn. We understood, however, that this was not the sign of sunrise, for whatever conditions might have prevailed on Venus eons ago, we were certain that the present condition of Venus meant endless night on one side and perpetual daylight on the other. According to our estimates, we were still about 800 miles away from the other side of Venus, so that perceiving sunrise from such a distance was an impossibility. My friend tried to provide us with a scientific explanation. Just as we can observe the first glimmer of dawn long before we see the sun, because the light gets reflected in the atmosphere in various ways, perhaps here too the light appeared due to such a process. Although it was scientific, I could not agree with my friend's viewpoint. If this was due to the atmosphere, we would have observed it even when we were in the caves 200 miles away. The atmosphere on Venus has a lower index of refraction compared to the Earth, therefore no such twilight appeared in the sky. The present debate remained unresolved. I thought of my aneroid barometer. It would have been useful at a time like this.

We increased our pace. The terrain was not rocky but flat, so we could move without much difficulty. The further we walked, the clearer the light in the sky became. The tranquil darkness of Venusian sky gradually turned pleasant and bright, and the stars in the firmament slowly began to disappear. Soon the light was strong enough for us to even see our shadow, and this thrilled us. After about twenty miles we observed a brilliant red line of light appear along the horizon. My friend initially thought it was the sun, but there was still a long way to go before we reached that point. But neither of us doubted anymore that it was indeed reflected sunlight. Our companion Ghatotkach began to shout, dance, and leap with such sudden enthusiasm that we wondered if he had gone crazy, and we began to prepare ourselves against a possible attack by this savage. But when he prostrated himself before us and began to thank us, we realized that he had not lost his mind after all. My friend had learned their language during our stay at the cave and explained it to me: "For Venusians this red light in the sky is regarded with great religious awe; the fortunate Venusian who has seen this great shrine even once in his life is respected in his community and also experiences great joy. Ghatotkach is thanking us for guiding him to this great shrine."

No longer was it necessary to compute our orientation, nor was it feasible in the absence of stars. We simply continued to walk in the direction of the red line in the distance. We did not, however, observe any difference in the overall illumination. We noticed instead something white in the distance after we had walked another day. We could not be certain as to what this was, but we speculated that it must be snow on a mountaintop. We realized that what we had observed so far was not the sun but its light reflected by the snow. The distant sight of this mountain prompted us to walk faster, and twenty hours later we were near enough to view it clearly.

We soon arrived at the foothills and started our ascent. The sublime magnificence of the mountain became immediately apparent. We decided to investigate the safest ways to traverse it, but my friend pointed out that crossing this mountain would be extremely dangerous—as it was formed not of rock, but only ice and snow. I did not pay heed to my friend's speculation initially but thought it merely the oddest of those odd notions he had been proposing throughout this trip. However, I soon realized he was right. We even discovered the reason for the mountain's existence. When the clouds on the brighter side of Venus travel towards the dark side, they come to a halt at the point where the temperature is cold enough to turn the water into snow and ice. Such precipitation over many eons had led to the formation of this ice mountain. The "ashen light" on Venus that many astronomers had seen from Earth was likely just a reflection from this mountain.

We began to think of ways in which we could accomplish our mission and reach the mountain's other side. Ghatotkach helped us greatly in our endeavors. His long claw-like fingers effortlessly dug into the snow, and after climbing a little distance he'd pull us up. Often, huge chunks of ice would topple from the mountaintop, and the frighteningly loud noises began to affect our hearing and our judgment. Yet the incessant efforts of Ghatotkach to scale the mountain and my friend's motivating words kept us going, and after a while we finally spotted the yellow-gold disk of the sun in the clear blue sky. However, our fear for our lives and the extreme cold kept us from appreciating its poetic beauty. It was only a matter of time, we thought, before we would be sent to our eternal rest by one of those chunks of ice plummeting from the mountaintop.

I do not know how far we had climbed by then, but I do remember that we had climbed to a very high point. From there we could see the other side of the mountain, but other than the great seas and many drifting icebergs we could spot nothing else. From where we stood, the path down the other side was a steep slope, but we realized it was not feasible to go downwards safely in that direction, nor was it possible to go anywhere else. Even Ghatotkach appeared stumped. My friend came up with an idea: We had brought with us a huge knife, which my friend gave it to Ghatotkach, demonstrating how he might carve hand- and toeholds in the ice that we could use to climb down. Ghatotkach followed his instructions, carving holds as he descended the far side of the mountain; noticing my fear, my friend followed him down first. After we had descended for a while, I abruptly lost my footing. My entire body trembled in fear as I slid down, frantically grabbing at my friend's leg, hoping that I could use it to balance myself again. But my friend could not bear my weight, so we both tumbled down the mountain, gaining speed as we went downhill. Ghatotkach started screaming, but soon the sound of strong wind drowned out this and every other noise. After about a minute we hit the sea below. Fortunately, there were no ice boulders below us, or else we would have been crushed. We both had good survival instincts, so we were able to rapidly scramble up onto a sheet of floating ice.

Our miraculous escape made us praise God and our good fortune. I was ashamed of having dragged my friend down with me and endangering his life. As for Ghatotkach, though he was an agile mountaineer we began to wonder what had become of him. Then, out of nowhere in this barren seascape, we heard a loud shout—and turned to find a group of men in a boat swiftly approaching us. Within minutes they were alongside us, and the men began to ask us questions eagerly. We could not understand their language, so we were unable to respond. But they made us board the boat without delay and swiftly maneuvered the narrow water passages between icebergs to bring us to a huge ship. Everyone aboard the ship was shocked to see us, but the captain offered us warm clothing and food. We were just as surprised to see these Venusians. They appeared completely human—in fact, the perfection of their lustrous black hair, bright shining eyes, and pleasant features would have been rare on Earth. Their dedication and mannerisms clearly indicated that they were an industrious advanced race. Every cabin aboard the ship had efficient heating arrangements and all the crew wore comfortable clothes woven from a cotton-like substance. We deduced, from their clothing, that they were inhabitants of a warmer climate.

We were curious as to the purpose of their travel to these frigid regions, and we subsequently learned that they were explorers on an official mission to uncover what was beyond the ice mountains. The ship had been about to get underway again on its voyage, but luckily for us they'd been delayed because one of their small boats had not yet made it back. My friend and I sat in a well-decorated room near a fireplace discussing our terrifying experiences so far on this planet. Interrupted by an agitated hubbub outside our door, we walked out to discover that the last boat had returned . . . bringing with it our obedient servant Ghatotkach. The ship's crew were taken aback by his behavior and did not know how to handle him. On spotting us, however, Ghatotkach started rolling at our feet in great delight. The captain, learning that this strange creature was our lowly companion, made arrangements for him as well. Later, we learned that, while inspecting the ice mountain, members of the crew of that boat had seen him screaming on a sheet of ice. Out of sympathy for his predicament, they had conveyed him aboard their boat.

The ship began moving swiftly in those narrow waters. Observing their competence in navigating such treacherous waters, we realized that they were a skilled seafaring race. We subsequently learned that this great ship ran on electricity alone, and that its capacity to support greater weight was due to its being crafted of aluminum or some such light material. Their navigating instruments left us in no doubt that this was a particularly civilized and advanced race; there was also ample evidence that they were more technologically advanced than earthlings even in their everyday lives. The captain, for example, took great care of us; his politeness and hospitality are something I will never forget. He was similarly attentive to the lowly Ghatotkach's needs. My friend sardonically commented that there was a reason for the captain's politeness. The fact that the ship headed home immediately after discovering us indicated that displaying us in their home country would bring them greater rewards than digging in the snow and ice would have done. Crossing the mountains was doubtlessly less prestigious than the discovery of a species. My friend had a point. We began to wonder what dangers lay ahead of us in our travels in Venus.

During our voyage, the captain would often visit us in his spare time, but the absence of a shared language made communication impossible. Sitting idly and leaving it all to fate was of little use, so we resolved to learn their language. The captain too expressed his interest in learning about us. We soon acquired the Venusian language thanks to his meticulous instruction.

As soon as we'd mastered their language we began to acquire greater evidence of their scientific and cultural development. In many branches of science, these Venusians were far superior than even modern Western science, though they had not made any significant advances in astronomy. Since it was perpetually daylight on their side of the planet, they had never had the opportunity to observe stars or other planets—only this could explain their lack of astronomical knowledge. In addition to the perpetual sunlight, the thick clouds that covered much of their sky also prevented them from learning about the cosmos, so they could hardly be blamed for their ignorance. They did possess a telescope and they had managed to observe Mercury, and even had charts on its transit. Because of their proximity to the Sun, they had greater knowledge of the Sun and its processes; however, because Venus had no moon, they had never observed a solar eclipse. Thus, they knew absolutely nothing about phenomena such as the stellar corona.

Their ignorance of astronomical phenomena made it exceedingly difficult to explain what we were. That there existed planets further from the Sun than Venus, such as Earth, was completely unknown to them, nor could we provide them with any proof. We had managed to convince them that we had come from the other side of the mountain with our companion, but the notion that we hailed from another planet was something they simply refused to entertain. They knew we were not from the sunlit portion of Venus, so they assumed us to be the inhabitants of their planet's other, dark side. We did manage to convince them eventually that we were not from the darker part, since we knew quite a bit about the Sun, and had in fact seen it, and had even studied solar phenomena such as 'sunspots' before. Eventually, and grudgingly, they admitted that our story about traveling from another planet might be true.

We were quite fascinated by the daily life of these Venusians—with their advanced culture and science. During the voyage, we were at first never gloomy. We engaged in a variety of activities and entertainments with the captain and crew. But my friend eventually became even more depressed than before, because all these happy activities reminded him of the life that he had left behind on Earth. One day after a meal, I was resting with my eyes closed in my small cabin when my friend slowly walked in and sat next to me. Finding me awake, he began to talk at length about the customs of these Venusians. It seemed he was particularly unhappy that day, so—without opening my eyes—I asked him the reason for this change in his mood. He explained it to me succinctly: "Whatever we'd wished to learn about life on the other side of Venus we already have learned on this ship, so there is simply no reason to continue this journey. We had so many expectations when we were journeying all those miles, but none of that enthusiasm remains with me. I am weary of this journey, and unhappy." As soon as he finished saying this, we suddenly noticed a flurry of activity and agitated voices outside the cabin.

I opened my eyes to investigate, and behold! I had returned to my old room on Earth. I realized that I had been on the couch all this while. The voices I had heard were none other than some sort of argument between my Odia and Bengali servants; although they received the same wages, they often argued over whose tasks and duties were more important. The argument today was no exception, but it was the reason my pleasant dream had come to an end. It was 8:00 at night, and a small lamp burned in one corner of the room. I also noticed that my friend was no longer in his armchair. I was curious to know what my friend had experienced while I was dreaming, so I left for his house without delay; I found him at home in an exuberant mood. When I learned that he knew nothing about the dream, though, I took leave of him; we could discuss my dream the following day. I was unable to sleep that night, and my wife must have thought I was unwell—but since I had slept during the day, I felt quite rested. In the morning I learned that my friend had received word the night before that he had been selected for a new job, so he had left the country immediately. Why had he not shared this news with me the night before? Mysterious. In any case, I have not shared the story of my strange dream with anyone . . . until today.

THE MYSTERY OF THE GIANT (1931)

Nanigopal Majumdar

1

We knew that May and June were the hottest months in Ranchi, but for some reason, my Dada [elder brother], my sister Habu, and I decided to visit the place in that scorching heat.

I have heard that the street in Ranchi where we lived that summer is now a proper road, fully paved. Back then it was just a bunch of white pebbles. I used to love that street. If you left the house and walked a little along the road, you would see several small and large hills; the tallest of them, Cave Hill, was said to have a lot of hidden caves. The thought of walking those hills on moonlit nights and soaking in the calm made me sigh with longing. Little did I know that the day I would get a chance to do so, my sighs would be filled with sadness instead.

The afternoons were for me to write fiction, and for Habu to play the children's game "daughter's wedding" with Auntie's daughter Bina. But Dada would always disappear at this hour. He would eat his lunch quickly and then rush out of the house. There was no deviation possible from this set routine. When Habu and Bina used to bother him every evening about why he wouldn't stay for their pretend wedding feast, Dada would laugh and say,

"I will, I will, just wait. Someone has already invited me to feast with them in the afternoons, so I won't be able to return in time for yours." Endlessly curious about his whereabouts, I'd ask, "Dada, where do you spend all your afternoons? If you stay at home, you can give me feedback on the plots of my new stories."

He'd respond by laughing. The laugh had only one meaning: "New authors are always interested in making others read their stuff." He'd say, his voice serious: "I spend my afternoons judging the worth of something far bigger than your stories. That work is almost finished, and hopefully soon it will be a lucky day for all of Bengal. It could be a fantastic day for the entire world, not just Bengal. As you know, I have a friend in these parts . . ." He'd abruptly cut his sentence short.

But one day Habu and Bina succeeded in blocking him from leaving. That day, they had a special wedding feast, and the two bridal parties had made a pact that the feast would be done by three in the afternoon. So Dada was stuck, but I noticed his extreme discomfort in staying put, as if his heart was in some other place in Ranchi.

Dada and I were sitting together that afternoon, when suddenly a terrifying noise shook the doors of the room, as if someone had just struck it with a large hammer. We were startled, and all of us stared at the door with trepidation. Why would anyone be pounding on our door? A minute passed, and then, again, the same terrifying bang! We heard a grotesque wailing sound, and the sound of shattering glass. Dada leaped to his feet and dashed towards the door.

The Odia gardener stood there, shivering and blue, as he said: "Babu, this is a calamity! I saw a spirit just now! He was as tall as two men, with a deformed face and a body covered in glass shards. He was completely naked except for a small loincloth. His body was totally white—he must be the spirit of a foreigner!"

I heard Dada, who was out of sight, say loudly: "Is that you? You?"

We heard a crashing sound, as if someone had silenced a roaring laugh with a single slap. So, did Dada recognize this "spirit"? How terrible! Was he practicing occult arts in secret all these afternoons? I had heard that if Yogis call upon spirits and demons but find no way to send them back to their realm, then evil will haunt them forever! Could it really be so?

I heard Dada's screams the next instant, and then heard something like a giant running away along the road. I followed the sound at once, but there was nothing to be seen, and no sign of Dada. My heart sank from fear, and I shouted out for him at the top of my lungs. But it was absolutely still. I ran down the street, straight towards the hills. In the distance, I saw a large dust cloud shaped like a human, maybe 10–12 feet high, appear and disappear on the hill.

Was it a human? Can there even be people who are this tall? Was this like those genies one reads about in the *Arabian Nights*? Did they kidnap Dada? And if so, why?

I returned home dejected and narrated the whole incident to my uncle. None of us could have imagined that we would face such a tragedy. My uncle was shocked: "This doesn't sound possible! Giants, demons, spirits, ghosts—such things do not exist in our day and age!" He asked for the gardener, who corroborated my account, swearing on Jagannath: "Yes indeed, Babu, it must be a spirit! He was twice as tall as you, and completely white! Some white sahib must have passed away in the madhouse, and this is his spirit."

Uncle replied: "So it's a madman?"

I interjected: "Madman? He is not even human! No human can be that tall!"

My uncle passed his fingers through his hair, and said, "Hmm, yes, and the most surprising thing are the last words you heard from your Dada. It makes me think that the two knew each other from before. But you think . . ."

By this time, Auntie, Habu, and Bina had heard the news and started crying, and neighbors had gathered as well. The story of the giant quickly spread through all of Ranchi. The police and the scientists heard our tale, but no one believed it. I sent a telegram to my father, who arrived the next day.

A search party was organized, and an investigation was launched into Dada's disappearance. Photos were published in newspapers, a reward was offered, yet nothing came of it at all. If only we had known where he used to spend his afternoons! But he had shared nothing with us, given no clues as to his activities. The sole development in the case only added to the mystery. It turned out that the same day Dada was kidnapped, another neighbor, Bangeshwar Talapatra, had also disappeared. We had little doubt that Bangeshwar babu had also fallen victim to the same giant. Bangeshwar babu was a renowned scholar who had devoted himself to scientific pursuits for the benefit of the nation. What could have prompted such a vicious attack on an innocent man? This was all a mystery!

2

Three days later. Our neighborhood had become the terror of Ranchi. Locals had seen a giant running in the hills in the dark, and they had also spotted a tiny figure with him. A few had even heard Sanskrit chants emanating from the hills late in the night. While the educated class tried to dismiss it all as mere superstition, the fear of the unknown gripped the entire town. We were convinced we would find Dada in those hills, but it was impossible to get there, since no one in town was brave enough to serve as our guide.

In the meantime, the mystery only kept deepening. Strange sounds had been heard at Bangeshwar babu's house at night, things had been moved around, strange whispers filled the air, footsteps that would chill the bone were heard. When the rumors grew, a policeman was dispatched to observe the place at night, but whatever he saw there made him faint—he was found unconscious on the street the next morning. He has suffered from a brain fever since then. However, whatever it was that he had encountered had not tried to hurt him; instead, one could tell from his wet clothes and other signs that whatever it was had tried to revive and minister to him. The same thing happened to the Santal woman two days ago, when she fainted close to the hills.

So who was it that was chanting in Sanskrit at night? Who lives in Bangeshwar babu's house? Could it be some benign, saintly spirit? Do spirits show such kindness towards humans? How did Dada come across such a spirit? And where did he and Bangeshwar babu disappear to?

Growing desperate, I decided that I would trek the hills myself, since that was the only way we would learn about Dada's fate. I slipped out of the house on a full-moon night. In the distance, the hill looked like a demon laughing with its teeth bare. It sent a shiver down my spine; I felt as if I could hear some deep breathing on my neck too. As I walked along, I sensed that I was being followed. I was too afraid to look behind me, so I picked up pace. A sad song from two voices floated in my ears, and it remains lodged in my brain to this day:

"A spirit am I not, nor a monster am I,
Listen to my tale, we are brothers, you and I!"

The voices came close to me, scaring me out of my wits. I looked up, fearfully, and oh what a sight! There loomed above me a gigantic creature, covered in fur, but its whole body was ghostly white. Next to it was another shadowy creature. Unable to comprehend what was happening, I ran like crazy back home and didn't stop till I was safely back inside. I still felt the song floating behind me: "Listen to my tale, we are brothers, you and I!"

3

I lay awake in bed next morning, wondering if the things I remembered from the night before were real or a nightmare. I could still hear the sad tune that had chased me through the dark. Just the memory of the giant and his shadowy companion made me shudder. When my father said that the police were no longer treating the incident as superstition, but were ready to go into the mountain that night to solve the mystery, my heart crumpled inside. "Listen to my tale, we are brothers, you and I!" But no one would have believed me, so I kept quiet.

Night fell again, and the moon was still just as bright. All of Ranchi seemed to have come alive, yet I could perceive its hidden grief. There were six of us: Dad, me, and four policemen. As we climbed, a sense of unease, as if something were missing, kept nagging at me. We had been on the path for a little while when a loud voice spoke in Hindi and startled all of us: "Come this way!" We saw a Sadhu sitting on a rock, quite able-bodied, with his face covered in a mass of hair. He said with a laugh: "I have been waiting for all of you!" He handed my dad an envelope, and then disappeared into a cave. We saw my brother's handwriting on the envelope. We opened it at once:

> Dear Father,
>
> I wanted to meet you once more, but it looks like it will no longer be possible. I left for the Himalayas today with the 'spirit.' I hope I will be able to help it.
>
> I met Bangeshwar Talapatra during my MSc studies at science college. He was the Zamindar of Shibrampur, with vast wealth and resources, and no family to speak of. He was extremely short, a little over four feet tall, and quite fair in complexion. But he had no peace of mind. He would often complain, woefully, "Manu, what is the point of having a

body like mine? I will develop something that will not just improve me but all Bengali people."

"How so?"

"I will create a potion that will once again transform us into the Aryans[1] of old: healthy, fit, and powerful."

This was his heart's desire. He came to Ranchi to conduct his experiments in peace. He did indeed succeed in creating a chemical potion that could transform birds and animals back to their giant, prehistoric shapes. The formula seemed to work on all kinds of animals: rats, frogs, cats and rabbits.

Talapatra then decided to experiment on himself. I said I would also try the potion. He refused to let me have any, saying that he had no idea what its effect on people might be, so he needed to test it first. He must have been a bit afraid of the experiment.

He took a dose, and immediately began to scream: "Manu, hold me, my head is bursting!" His face and eyes turned blood-red, and he slumped to the floor holding his head. I put him to bed and left for home. The next day when I visited him, I saw that his whole body had swollen quite a bit, and he had also grown a bit taller. He could not speak at all; he would open his mouth and something glass-like would come out of it; if he threw it out with his hand, his mouth would fill up once again with the same substance. I returned home wondering whether I should find him a doctor or leave it up to nature to heal him. The next day I was stuck at home when all of a sudden we heard a loud knock. It was Talapatra—or rather something that looked like him. He was three times as tall as he used to be, and his mouth and body were covered in shards of glass. I was shocked. He tried to say something, then hoisted me up and began running off instead. Uff, it was insane! No, Talapatra was insane!

He stopped in front of a cave in the hill. I realized that although he had not gone completely crazy, his brain power had definitely decreased. Even so, he must have realized that he was now an exile from civilization. Humans would no longer accept him in their midst, so he wanted to find a space where he would no longer be seen by human eyes. He had abducted me because I was the only one who knew of his pain. After about three days, he began to recover his voice, and his mouth no longer spit glass. He explained that his potion had mixed with the chemicals of his body and transformed into a new chemical, one that affected his glands and turned him into a giant. This new chemical also oozed out of his body, in sweat and saliva, turning into a glass-like substance upon exposure to the air. This was why he had been unable to speak for the first few days.

I could not help but cry at his plight. It was tragic to see that this man, who had wanted to help all of humanity, had turned into a monstrous creature. For a few nights, we searched his home laboratory in search of a cure, and everyone thought we were spirits. He was afraid of being seen by humans, hence we had to work in secret. If the hills had not been full of ripe fruit we would not be alive to share this tale.

Soon I sensed a new danger. Talapatra's body had grown with the potion indeed, but his brain had not grown with it. He had great difficulty comprehending things, and soon I realized that he was losing his mind entirely. There was not much semblance left of a human brain anymore in that shell. I was wondering what to do with him when God sent me a solution to the problem. I met a Sadhu, who heard my tale and revealed that there was a type of root to be found in the Himalayan mountains whose juice would surely heal

Talapatra and return him to normal. I noted down all the details of this medicine, entrusted this letter to the Sadhu, and we departed for the Himalayas. I feel honor-bound to help Talapatra, as I feel responsible for his fate. My respects to you, dear father.

Yours affectionately,
Manu

Our eyes welled up in tears reading this account. In the distance, we saw a giant leaping from slope to slope, carrying an ordinary-sized man on his shoulders.

THE MARTIAN PURANA (1931)[1]

Manoranjan Bhattacharya

All the servants and valets, boys and butlers of Kaurava Lodge[2] wore a worried look on their faces.

What seems to be the matter? Are the Kauravas and Pandavas going to war again? No, that cannot be. The League of Nations has issued notices on Bhima and Arjuna, so although they are allowed to hunt a few small birds for sport, if they were to draw the Gandiva for war, or the great mace, all people would go on a hunger strike. Lest all these people die from their hunger strike, the lord of Dharma, Yudhisthira, has deposited the Gandiva at the Imperial Bank. He was too afraid to lock it up at home. Who knows when Bhima might get angry? If he does, then no lock can stop him![3]

So why is everyone so agitated? Well, there is a bit of back-story which you need to know at this point. It has been five days since Subhadra returned from her parental home, and due to last-minute packing she had taken her brother Krishna's syamantaka gem with her by mistake. Now there was a party at the Kaurava lodge the next day, and Subhadra, being a woman, could not resist putting it on. And then of course the great glow of the gem astounded everyone and became the focus of attention. Duryodhana's wife became extremely jealous at this—even the taste of delicious Bhimnag *sandesh* seemed like quinine to her. When the Pandavas finally left in their Rolls Royce, she locked herself into her *gosaghar*.[4]

Soon Duryodhana got to hear of all this, and being the proud man that he is, it fanned the flames of his anger. He promised his wife that he would get a gemstone within a week, one whose shine would far surpass that of Keshta's syamantaka.[5] He didn't want his wife locking herself up in her chamber and sleeping on its cold floor, as there had been many cases of influenza in town recently.

That very day Duryodhana sent a broker to Vasuki, lord of nagas[6] in the underworld, to inquire whether he would sell him the glowing *Nagamani* gemstone from his own head, or failing that an equally rare and valuable serpent's ornament. Of course, he was ready to offer a good price for it. The messenger returned with the news that the Electric Corporation had, out of sheer laziness, not yet managed to install power lines in the underworld. What little kerosene was available had been taken away by the American Rockefeller on the one side and the Burmah Oil Company[7] on the other. So if the nagas sold their gemstones then the underworld would be in darkness. It was therefore impossible to sell any serpent's gem. However, the king of nagas did have a tip for Duryodhana. In recent years, taxes had increased so much in Europe that even the rich lords and ladies had been forced to pawn their jewelry to Lord Kubera. Thus Kubera might have a few choice gems he could possibly sell off.[8]

Duryodhana called up Kubera immediately and learned that Lord Penny-Wanting's three famous jewels, 'Matchless,'

‘Priceless,’ and ‘Worthless,’ had all been pawned to Kubera. While the first two had already been sold off once Penny-Wanting proved unable to redeem them, the third, ‘Worthless’, the only truly valuable one of the three, was still available for sale. After quite a bit of haggling they decided on a price, and Jayadratha and Bhurishrava left in an airplane for Alka.[9]

However, the two failed to return on time. From Alka came the news that they had indeed taken ‘Worthless’ and left. When it became clear after a week that the two would not return, Duryodhana approached the Sahadeva Institute, which was not an investigative agency but a club of astrologers. After being awarded the Nobel Prize, the famous astrologer Dr. Sahadeva had established this institute on a mountaintop in peaceful cold Kasauli.[10] Dr. Sahadeva usually stayed in Hastinapur, but he visited the institute every once in a while to direct its affairs.[11]

The Institute’s report was quite mysterious. Apparently the stone was no longer on Earth but on Mars. On their way back from Alka, Jayadratha and Bhurishrava had decided to trek over the Everest, but they had lost the ‘Worthless’ on the way. Out of shame, the two were no longer able to return to Hastinapur. How the stone had reached Mars the astrologers could not say. Duryodhana buried his head in his hand in dismay upon hearing this.

While all this was going on, the *Hastinapur Times* published strange and unexpected news. It had long been proposed by scientists that Mars was likely the home of a highly advanced species. Compared to Martians, humans were like children. It was therefore essential for humanity's development that contact should be established between the two. The scientists had theorized that a rocketship could be built that would carry humans, and this was to be shot from a cannon to Mars, and thus it would be possible for humans to meet Martians. Vishwakarma and Co. had been given the order to create this rocket, and they had built it already. All that was left to decide was who would embark on this mission.[12]

Duryodhana read the news a couple of times before it dawned on him that it was as if God himself had created this opportunity for him to recover the gem. If he sent one of his own people along with the rocket's crew, it would be perfect. Of course, his cousin Vrikodara was the best person for the job, but would he agree? They had been rivals since childhood. So Duryodhana pressed the bell on his desk a few times to call his attendant, and sent for Dushasana.[13]

Dushasana arrived in a few moments. Duryodhana asked him, hesitantly: "Hey Dushu, have you seen today's paper?"

Dushasana replied immediately: "Of course, dada! Not only did I see it, I sent a wireless to book a seat for myself on that rocket. What better opportunity to snub those Pandavas! When we return from Mars everyone will sing our praises. Then Arjuna's Olympic medals and Sahadev's Nobel will all appear insignificant!"

Duryodhana lifted his younger brother in delight. After a few more words, Duryodhana added, casually, almost as if it was an afterthought: "By the way, Dushu, your sister-in-law's new gem, 'Worthless,' seems to have reached Mars by mistake. See if you can get it back?"

Dushasana responded: "Don't worry, brother! I will get that stone as well."

Lest their mother Gandhari interrupt their plans, the two brothers contrived to send her on a pilgrimage to Rameshwaram with Uncle Shakuni. The blind king Dhritarashtra protested the plan, but he was calmed down by the brothers' reassurance. After about fifteen days, the *Hastinapur Times* carried a new headline, and the paperboy loudly announced it: "The Mission to Mars! Dushu Raja goes to Mars! Big news, babu!" and so on.[14]

Several days after the rocket's launch, there was still no news from Mars. Whether the highly intelligent beings were pleased to see humans, whether the rocket had indeed reached Mars and not been burnt to ashes on the way, nobody could say. Once again the astrologers of Sahadeva Institute were consulted, and they gave their report in two days. The rocket had indeed reached Mars, but its passengers were in great trouble. That is all their science could tell.

When the news reached Kaurava Lodge, everything turned upside-down. Gandhari had returned from her pilgrimage, and on hearing this began to have regular fainting spells. And Dhritarashtra's blood pressure rose so high that Yudhisthira had to keep Ghatotkach on emergency alerts, so that the latter could get visalyakarani from the Ghandamadan mountain if necessary.[15]

A few more days passed like this, but there was still no news from Mars. Finally, when she could stand it no longer,

Gandhari approached Bhima and said: "Please, son, save this mother of yours[16], bring back my Dushasana. There is nothing your brother Hanuman cannot do, please ask him for me. For Lord Rama he once leaped to Lanka, so for me perhaps he would go to Mars. By Sita-devi's boon he is immortal and invulnerable. He still retains all his strength. Please, my son, request him on my behalf."[17]

Bhima reached Kishkindha the following afternoon, and learnt that his elder brother had retired to a "Kala-Bhavan." Bhima at first assumed that his brother had after retirement began to pursue the arts. If he had built an art academy, would he still be willing to jump like other ordinary monkeys as he did in the old days?

His fears went away the moment he approached Hanuman's house, which in fact had nothing to do with art; instead, it was a banana orchard.[18] On all sides one could see every variety of banana—chanpa, martaman, kanthali, agnishwar, and others—and in the midst of it all sat the son of the Wind-god, Hanuman himself, eating his *kala*. Next to him lay a small mound of banana peels.

Bhima peeked in and said in a low voice: "Brother . . ."

"Who is it?" asked Hanuman, and turned to find Bhima. With great delight Hanuman invited him in, and made him feast on a lot of martaman bananas. After this warm reception, he asked: "So what brings you here?"

"I come to you in dire need, brother. You know that rocket that went to Mars? My cousin Dushasana was on it. It has been quite a while and we still have not heard from him. The astrologers tell us that he is in trouble. Elder mother has all but given up eating, and sent me to ask whether you could go to Mars in this age as you did before in the *Treta yuga*[19], and find a solution to it all."

Hanuman lazily stretched himself and said: "It has been thousands of years, brother. I have given up jumping about totally. In fact, ever since the railways came to Kishkindha I have almost given up walking as well. Now I have a pot belly. I am no longer able to do such marvelous things."

Bhima was no foolish youngster. He knew that Hanuman would say such things at the beginning, but if he was pressed harder he would agree. He said: "So what if you have a pot belly? A couple days of exercise on the parallel bars, along with a dozen weight-loss pills, and you will be just as before."

Of course, elder siblings can never win an argument against their younger siblings, and Hanuman could not either. So he decided to jump to Mars after thousands of years of retirement. After a pilgrimage to Rameshwaram, where he prayed to Lord Rama, he leaped into the sky with a huge cry, a cry that rocked all the Earth, even Bhima.

Hanuman was entranced by the lovely vision of Mars. Earth seemed so dirty in comparison. A pleasant wind blew all over the planet, and if one listened to it carefully it seemed as if music itself had been woven on these winds. Such was the great skill of these Martians. On Earth everything was so difficult! Even getting proper food required such labor: plant seeds, wait for the crop to ripen, cut them, cook them! Here there was no such need. Huge trees were planted all around, and on their branches hung all kinds of delicacies, from cutlets to cake, toffee to cheese! And one did not even need to struggle to pluck them. There were different switches on the ground which one could press to get different items. Hanuman had pushed a yellow one experimentally, and he was given a whole bunch of bananas! Oh, if humans could learn such art from these intelligent creatures, there would be no food problems on Earth! Surely the rocket had not reached Mars, for would not such intelligent creatures wish to know about humans as well?

Hanuman had spotted a few round footballs in the distance, but on coming closer he realized that these were the Martians. After thousands of years of evolution, it seemed they had lost the need for limbs; all that had grown was the head. There were two small legs beneath each giant head, and that was all they seemed to require.

When Hanuman realized that these were the Martians, he did not present himself to them immediately, but hid and observed them by assuming the form of a small monkey, the same disguise he had used in Ashokavana while trying to find Sita. Then he leaped from tree to tree, and eventually came to a huge garden.

There were hundreds of cages in this small garden, and there were many strange creatures inside each of these. Hanuman realized he had come to a zoological garden. After wandering about for a bit, Hanuman observed that there was one particular cage that attracted the largest crowd. Thinking it must contain some fantastic species, Hanuman leaned closer. It seemed this was feeding time, and some Martian youngsters also seemed to be poking the creatures inside with sticks. Highly intrigued, Hanuman tried to find out from his hiding place in the trees what these creatures looked like. But he could not see very clearly. He figured that the zoo would close soon as it was almost evening, and perhaps he could take a closer look when the visitors had left. Soon it was evening, and the zoo closed for the day. When it was dark, Hanuman came down from the tree and approached the cage. What a surprise! It was Dushasana and the other missing humans.

Hanuman and Dushasana knew each other. Quickly assuming his proper form, Hanuman asked: "Dushasana! How did you get caught in this mess?"

Dushasana was no less surprised to see Hanuman. Almost in tears, he said: "Oh dada! What can I say—we had come to initiate contact with these intelligent beings, and they thought we were only strange animals and locked us up in this zoo. Thousands of visitors come to see us every day. The more we try to explain, the more they laugh and poke us with sticks. They have almost made a hole in Dr. Goyter's stomach with their poking!"

At first Hanuman was so angry, that if any of these humans had held a matchstick, he could have set the zoo ablaze. But he came to realize that these Martians were highly intelligent creatures who had great scientific knowledge, so mere strength would not work against them. Lest they also capture him and put him in a cage, he whispered to the captives: "Grab hold of my tail, or tie it to the bars of the cage. I will jump again and carry you back to Earth."

Notes

The Inhumans (1935)

1. Odias: the inhabitants of the Odisha state in India.

2. Marwaris: an Indian ethnic group that originates in Rajasthan, but who are renowned for their business acumen. They occupy a special niche among Bengali trading communities.

3. Lake Bunyonyi lies in south-western Uganda, between Kisoro and Kabale.

4. Paul Graetz (1875–1968), sometimes called the "German Indiana Jones," was the first to travel across Africa by motorcar.

5. W. Robert Foran, *Kill or Be Killed: The Rambling Reminiscences of an Amateur Hunter* (1933). I have used the original text by Foran rather than translating Roy's (slightly condensed) translation back into English.

6. Valakhilyas are a group of thumb-high sages described in Hindu Puranic and epic literature.

7. Jujus are imaginary creatures common in Bengali lore, associated with evil and magic.

8. The Opium trade established by the British played a significant role in the economic impoverishment of Bengal in the nineteenth century. In referring to the opium eater's dream, moreover, Roy was signaling a tradition of tall tales in Bengal written by writers such as Bankim Chandra Chattopadhyay and Trailokyanath Mukhopadhyay, in which opium users would tell fanciful stories in their drug haze.

9. Prince Vijaya (543–505 BC) is a legendary figure in various South Asian chronicles. He is regarded as the first king of Sri Lanka and the originator of the Sinhalese people.

10. This is an example of Roy's wordplay. The word *chandra* means "moon," and the people of the land are moon-faced.

11. Shastras are written knowledge sources, everything from philosophical treatises to technical and practical manuals.

12. Ravana is the king of Sri Lanka, presented as a demon or *rakshasa* in the Hindu epic *Ramayana*. The primary antagonist in the epic, Ravana is also depicted in the same sources as a learned scholar, a devotee of the lord Shiva. Ravana is worshiped in numerous parts of South and Southeast Asia.

13. Amal and Amala are male and female versions of the same name.

14. Bhang is a cannabis drink, common in South Asia as a celebratory drink.

15. *Dada* means elder brother in Bangla. It is also a common mode of respectful but endearing address.

16. An expert musician.

17. A tabla is a pair of twin drums, commonly used in South Asian music.

Voyage to Venus (1895)

1. *Amrita* is a mythical elixir in Puranic mythology, consumed by the gods.

2. Ghatotkach is a mythological character from the Sanskrit epic *Mahabharata*. He is the son of Pandava Bhima, a half human-half deity figure, and Hidimba, a demoness.

The Mystery of the Giant (1931)

1. "Aryans" are ancient Indo-Iranian people. The Sanskrit word "Arya" designates the ethnocultural group of Vedic Sanskrit speakers, while Aryavarta is a name used in different Sanskrit texts to designate the Indian subcontinent. The use of the term in twentieth-century Nazi ideology was a colonial appropriation of the concept.

The Martian Purana (1931)

1. The story uses characters and plot details from two Hindu epics: the *Mahabharata* and the *Ramayana*. It is the former that is the main focus in this story. Briefly summarized, the story details the struggle for power between two branches of the same family: the Pandavas and the Kauravas. The Pandavas are five semi-divine brothers. The *Mahabharata* is a bloody tale which has at its core the battle of Kurukshetra, in which the Pandavas emerge victorious after killing the Kauravas and their allies.

2. The demotion of the palace of the Kauravas to a mere lodge signals that this will not be a traditional *Purana*. A Purana, literally meaning "ancient," is a repository of Hindu myths and legends.

3. Gandiva is Arjuna's bow. Arjuna is one of the Pandavas and a renowned archer. Bhima, another Pandava, whose preferred weapon is the mace, is the strongest man in the *Mahabharata* universe. Yudhisthira, the eldest of the Pandavas, is the son of the god Dharma (law and ethics), and an embodiment of its principles.

4. Subhadra is the half-sister of Krishna and the wife of Arjuna. Krishna is regarded as an avatar of Vishnu, one of the Hindu trinity, and a central character in the *Mahabharata* universe. The syamantaka is a famous gem that was given to Krishna. Duryodhana, while not the leader of the Kauravas, is the chief antagonist of the Pandavas, so his death brings the battle of Kurukshetra to an end. Bhimnag *sandesh* are regarded as a particularly delicious candy. The chamber of anger ("*gosaghar*") is a place where women would withdraw to express their resentment and anger, but it is more of a comic concept.

5. Keshta is Krishna, but it is a vulgar and humourous use.

6. Nagas are mythological half-human, half-serpent deities that reside in the underworld. They are a common part of folklore and mythology in the Indian subcontinent.

7. Burmah Oil Company was a leading British oil company, which had a near-monopoly on oil trade in South and Southeast Asia during the colonial period.

8. Kubera is the lord of wealth in Hindu mythology.

9. Jayadratha and Bhurishrava are both allies of the Kauravas in the battle of Kurukshetra.

10. Kasauli is a town and cantonment in the Indian state of Himachal Pradesh. It is a popular tourist destination.

11. Sahadeva is the youngest and most intelligent of the five Pandavas.

12. Vishwakarma is the great architect of the universe and a master builder.

13. Dushasana is a younger brother of Duryodhana. Vrikodara is another name for Bhima.

14. Gandhari, the Queen, is the wife of the blind king Dhritarashtra and the mother of Duryodhana. Shakuni, her brother, is also a mentor of the Kauravas; he is often seen as the archetype of the evil uncle in Hindu mythology.

15. Ghatotkach is the son of Bhima. Vishalyakarani is a medicinal plant used in Ayurveda.

16. While Gandhari is the in-law paternal aunt, within the kinship system of Hindus, she is given the same status as the mother, and is often referred to as the elder or senior mother.

17. Hanuman, son of the god of Wind, and half brother of Bhima, is a white monkey. He is a central character in the Hindu epic *Ramayana*, or the epic of Rama. Sita-devi or Sita is the wife of Rama.

18. This is a play on words: The term *kala* in Sanskrit refers to the arts, while in Bangla it refers to bananas.

19. *Treta* is the second of the four *Yugas*, or great cycles of time, in Hindu mythology. The events in the *Ramayana* are set in the *Treta yuga*, while the *Mahabharata* is set in the third, *Dwapar yuga*.

Bodhisattva Chattopadhyay is Associate Professor in Global Culture Studies at the Department of Culture Studies and Oriental Languages, University of Oslo, and series editor of Routledge's *Studies in Global Genre Fiction*. The leader and sole-PI of CoFUTURES, a global sf initiative funded by the European Research Council and Norwegian Research Council, and producer of the documentary *Kalpavigyan: A Speculative Journey* (2021), which charts the history of Bangla sf, Chattopadhyay is the recipient of numerous prizes, including the World Fantasy Award in 2020.

Manoranjan Bhattacharya (1903–1939) was a fiction writer, translator, and editor who contributed extensively to children's and young adult literature. He is particularly known for editing the magazine *Ramdhanu*, which served as one of the main periodicals via which Bangla SF took shape.

Nanigopal Majumdar (1897–1938) was an Indian archaeologist and Sanskrit scholar. Known among archaeologists as NGM, he is credited with having discovered numerous Indus Valley Civilization sites.

Jagadananda Ray (1869–1933) was a Bengali science writer and author. His story "Voyage to Venus" (1895) was one of the earliest scientific romance stories written in Bangla.

Hemendrakumar Roy (1888–1963) is a founding figure for Bangla sf as a writer, editor, and translator. "Hemen Roy" also wrote social realist fiction and non-sf genre fiction, not to mention essays on Bengali culture, popular science, and art. Via sf, he popularized scientific and technological breakthroughs and promoted an anti-colonial vision . . . while criticizing the excesses of nationalist chauvinism. Roy continues to be one of the most widely read figures in Bangla literature.